"Jake, I have to talk t... everything's going w... with my mother, and ... paper for class, and I don't know what to do."

Kate felt like she was losing control. Words were just pouring out of her mouth. She didn't even know if she made any sense, and Jake didn't respond. Is he mad at me? She searched her memory, urgently trying to recall the last time she'd talked to him. He had been so sweet then. He hadn't seemed angry at all. What was going on?

"Kate," he said. "Can we talk about this later?"

Titles in the MAKING OUT series

And more fabulous MAKING OUT books will follow!

Kate finds love

KATHERINE APPLEGATE

Pan Books

Cover photography by Jutta Klee

First published 1997 by Macmillan Children's Books
a division of Macmillan Publishers Limited
25 Eccleston Place, London SW1W 9NF
and Basingstoke

Associated companies throughout the world

ISBN 0 330 35114 1

1 3 5 7 9 8 6 4 2

A CIP catalogue record for this book is available from
the British Library.

Printed and bound in Great Britain by
Mackays of Chatham plc, Kent

For Michael

Zoey

It's hard to imagine what Benjamin sees when he sees me. I guess it must be kind of a shock for him. I mean, the last time he saw me I was eleven, with a mouth full of metal and rubber bands. I hadn't even thought about shaving my legs, and I wore T-shirts with slogans like I'm with Stupid on them.

Well, I definitely don't wear the dumb T-shirts anymore, and I don't have the mouth full of metal. (I still have a trace of buck teeth. I know, I know, blame my orthodontist. All those years with a night brace and for what?) So I guess when it comes down to it, I'm the same old Zoey, just a little bit taller, with a figure and a tiny bit more fashion and cosmetic sense.

Still, I wonder if what Benjamin sees when he sees me is Zoey, the adult who's about to go to college. Or if he sees me as something else. Zoey, the kid sister who's just a little less gawky than she used to be and somehow — miraculously — has a boyfriend and a life.

It's weird to think that everything that's old to me is new to Benjamin — like how Mom changed the kitchen a couple of years back, or how we got all new television sets two years ago, or how we now have yellow tile in the bathroom instead of blue.

Sometimes we'll be sitting there at dinner with Mom and Dad or something, and I'll catch Benjamin just staring. What is it that he's looking at? Is it that Mom and Dad look so much older? Is it that I don't look like the sister he imagined?

Do I look like a stranger to him?

Kate

Sometimes I wake up in the middle of the night, and the dream I've had is so powerful, I don't know how I'm ever going to get it out of my head.

It's the same dream I've had since prom night, and the truth is, it's not really a dream, it's more like a nightmare.

I'm driving in the Cabrals' car, wearing my dressiest outfit, thinking that I'm about to have the best night with the best guy, when suddenly I see in the rearview mirror that there's a car behind me. And

inside the car is a girl. She's
staring at me in this really
haunting way. Like she's got a
purpose. As the car gets closer
to me I recognize the girl. I
try to stop what I know is
about to happen, but I'm
completely helpless. Time stands
still for a second, then
everything goes black.

   That's usually when I wake
up, sit upright in my bed, my
hair wet with perspiration, my
hands shaking, only to realize
that the nightmare I had
really happened a little over a
week ago and that I know who
the girl is. . . . It's Lara
McAvoy, and she ran me off

the road on my way to the prom.

I get up, slip on my robe, and go to the Cabrals' kitchen. I get a glass of water, and sit at the kitchen table, and remind myself I'm fine, I survived, I didn't really get hurt. And Lara McAvoy is gone. Or temporarily gone at least, at a drug rehabilitation center her dad took her to. And Jake is here on Chatham Island. With me.

When I get back in bed, I have a technique that always puts me back to sleep. I pretend I'm shooting a roll of film and that Jake's my subject. We're outside at the beach, and he's walking around, striking different poses, mugging for the camera. I'm snapping pictures the whole time, laughing as I go in close on his face and focus in on his eyes, so soft and brown.

I fall asleep to the click of my imaginary camera, to the image of Jake, and everything's all right.

The administration and faculty of Weymouth High School extend a warm welcome to family and friends as we honor our graduating seniors and bid them a fond farewell.

Please join us for a postceremony reception on the football field directly after the proceedings.

One

Zoey Passmore looked at her watch. *Only fifteen minutes until I'm a high-school graduate,* she thought, taking a deep breath and repositioning herself in her chair. She fiddled with the gold-and-silver chain-link bracelet she wore around her right wrist and tried not to look at her watch again.

It was hard to believe this day was finally upon her, but here she was—sitting in the most uncomfortable folding chair on earth, on what felt like the hottest day Chatham Island had seen all year, her legs itching under the graduation gown she was wearing—waiting for her life to change.

It was funny, but Zoey had spent so much time imagining what her graduation would be like, and she'd never had any idea how she'd actually feel. All the scenarios she'd envisioned had her feeling a little relieved, and even a little nostalgic, but none of them had her feeling like she did right

9

now: like nothing would ever be the same again.

"If there's one thing I can leave you with, it's that you should always follow your dreams," the principal was saying as he closed his speech, his voice resonating across the football field. *What's wrong with me?* Zoey reprimanded herself as she felt herself tearing. *I can't believe I'm letting the principal's speech get to me even a little bit.*

Zoey turned her head to see if Aisha Gray, who was sitting directly behind her, was having a similar reaction. But of course Aisha, pragmatic as ever, was just staring straight ahead, as if she were listening to a physics lecture or a seminar on how to take your SATs.

Zoey whipped around toward the audience, the tassel on her graduation cap hitting her on the side of the head. She scanned the crowd for her best friend, Nina Geiger. The minute Zoey's eyes met Nina's, her friend crinkled up her nose disdainfully and gave a roll of her eyes that read: *Can you believe this cheese fest?*

Zoey turned back around. *Just wait until it's Nina's turn,* she thought. *She'll see what it's like.* Nina was a year younger than Zoey; a year younger than most of her friends. She had a whole year at Weymouth High School

10

to go, and she'd already made it clear that she was not exactly thrilled to be left behind.

Zoey felt on a tap on her shoulder. It was Aisha. "Look, they're handing out the awards," she muttered under her breath. Zoey sat up in her chair. "Of course, it's David Barnes," Aisha said, sighing. "You better believe he got the science award."

Zoey shot Aisha a comforting glance. After all, this couldn't be easy for her. Not so much because Aisha had wanted to win the science award herself, which she had. But because it probably wasn't very easy to see David Barnes after what had happened at the prom. Zoey couldn't help thinking: *I told you not to bring two dates with you; I told you that you'd get busted. If you had listened to me, everything would have worked out.*

Then again, Zoey figured, as far as Aisha was concerned, everything really had worked out for the best. In that inimitable Aisha fashion she'd managed somehow to extricate David Barnes from her life, and now she and Christopher Shupe, her long-lost fiancé, were engaged to be married.

Zoey got a chill just thinking of one of her good friends getting married. She couldn't even begin to consider that for herself right now. Of course, in the back of her head she hoped that Lucas Cabral would be the guy she spent the rest of her life with, but she wasn't delusional. She knew that a lot could happen in the next four years. Lucas was forever drumming it into her head that distance would change things, and with her at the University of California at Berkeley and him at the University of Maine, there was certainly going to be a lot of distance between them.

Lucas was sitting a couple of rows back and to the left. Zoey tried to catch his eye, but he was staring rigidly toward the ground. Zoey felt a pang in her stomach. *What's wrong with him?* she wondered. Lucas had arrived at graduation late, and he had remained sitting in a slumped position the whole time. Even now Zoey could only see his blond head, bowed down between his shoulders.

Should I get out of my seat and go over to him? Zoey wondered. *Or would I just be making a scene?* She couldn't imagine what was wrong with Lucas, unless what was bothering him was the same thing that had been bothering him for the past few months: that she'd be going away to California and he'd be staying here in Maine. *But we have the whole summer in front of us,* Zoey thought.

She sighed and looked up at the stage.

Claire Geiger was receiving her award for being class valedictorian. Zoey was struck by how good she looked: The graduation gown actually looked flattering on her tall figure, and her long black hair was glistening in the sun as she moved gracefully from faculty member to faculty member, shaking each one of their hands.

Zoey looked at her watch again and then at the program. If Claire was up there now, giving her acceptance speech, that meant that handing out diplomas was the next order of business. Zoey began to prepare herself for the trip up to the stage. She reapplied some lip gloss she had in her bag and combed down her dark blond hair as she listened to the principal rattle off the names of students, going alphabetically down the list.

"Lucas Cabral!" the principal called out, and Zoey shot to attention. She jumped out of her seat and gave a loud whoop. Lucas turned, and when their eyes met, she saw his wry half smile and felt a warm shudder run through her body. He was still hers. She watched as Lucas went to get his diploma, and she tried to make eye contact with him again as he stepped down from the stage. "I love you," she mouthed, but this time he wasn't looking.

Zoey craned her neck to watch Lucas as he resumed his seat and his same slumped position. By the time she turned back toward the stage, the principal was already on the *P*'s. Zoey shuffled in her seat and did her best to regain her focus.

"Benjamin Passmore," the principal boomed.

As Benjamin made his way up to the stage Zoey could feel the tears start to come again. Her brother was walking proudly toward the principal, his head held high, his beautiful brown eyes focused in front of him. Wasn't it only a few weeks ago that Benjamin wouldn't leave the house without his Ray-Ban sunglasses on? Wasn't it only a few weeks ago that Benjamin was still afflicted with blindness? Since the age of fourteen Benjamin's world had been a dark one, and now—thanks to a medical miracle—a light had been rekindled for him. He was a whole new person with the whole world before his eyes. Zoey's body tingled as Benjamin made his way down the stage, a broad smile on his face. The sporadic clapping and catcalls from the audience erupted into thunderous applause.

"Zo, get ready," Aisha muttered, tapping furiously on Zoey's shoulder.

"Zoey Passmore," boomed the principal.

Zoey stood up to get her diploma. Out of

the corner of her eye she caught a glimpse of Lucas. He was edging his way out of the rows of folding chairs, walking away from the ceremony alone.

Kate Levin felt her stomach twitch as Coach McNair presented the Athlete of the Year award to Jake McRoyan.

"Jake McRoyan is a model athlete and a model individual, a tribute to Weymouth High School," Coach McNair bellowed, his voice shaky with emotion. "We will all miss him terribly when he's off at the University of Massachusetts, although they will be lucky to have an athlete like him."

Miss him? I don't know how I'll live without him, Kate thought mournfully. She wondered if Jake could see her from the stage, and then she gave her outfit the once-over to make sure she looked passably okay. *This is probably too much,* Kate thought as she brushed her skirt down with her hands. She'd opted to wear a long, straight tan linen skirt over which she wore a white button-down shirt and a navy blue cotton cardigan. It seemed like an appropriate enough outfit, kind of preppy and kind of dressy. But being from the city, Kate still felt like an outsider, and she was never sure if she had Chatham Island protocol down pat. Sometimes she wondered if the Chatham Island residents thought she was trying too hard.

Not that Jake ever made Kate feel anything but completely comfortable. He was so good at putting her at ease. He wasn't the kind of guy who was embarrassed to show affection. He always held her hand in public, always kissed her good-bye even if other people were around.

She focused in on him. He looked so humble, standing next to Coach McNair, waiting to accept his award. Kate loved the way you could see the outline of Jake's athletic build underneath his cap and gown, and she found his awkwardness—how he kept his head down the whole time Coach McNair spoke, how he kept shuffling around as if he couldn't wait for all the praise to stop—incredibly endearing.

Mrs. Cabral was seated next to Kate, and she turned to Kate to whisper: "He seems sweet, your new boyfriend." Kate reached for her hand and squeezed it.

Kate felt a glow of warmth wash over her, like she sometimes felt after working out. Everything was okay. She had a good home, a boyfriend, and, of course, her photography. The art school she attended in Weymouth had some incredible course offerings and some amazing visiting professors coming in from different universities for the summer classes.

Kate reached into her bag and felt around for her camera. *I should have been taking photos the whole time*, she realized. She dug her sandals into the ground at the thought of all the good shots she could have gotten. So what if some of them were a little cliché? She could have done something cool with the lighting and the shadows to make the shots work. At least she could have gotten a shot of Lucas as he shook the principal's hand or Jake as he accepted his award.

Kate rummaged around the bag in a desperate search for her camera. But all she came up with was her wallet and her lip balm. Could she have forgotten to put her camera in her bag? It wasn't possible. She searched some more, patting the damp ground beneath her chair to see if perhaps the camera had fallen out of her bag.

Kate felt her body freeze. She was so absentminded sometimes, so clueless. How could she not have brought her camera? She felt lost without it.

Kate could hear the glee club harmonize as they performed the Weymouth High School anthem, and she tried to let the music seep into her, ease her mind, but it didn't work. As if Mrs. Cabral could feel the change in Kate, she leaned over and put her arm around her. "Sometimes these ceremonies make me emotional, too," she whispered in Kate's ear.

"Ladies and gentlemen," the principal boomed, "let's give the graduating class a big round of applause!"

Kate watched as the class threw their caps in the air. *That would have been a good shot,* she thought.

Claire

I admit, I've wondered what Benjamin thinks of my appearance now that he has his sight back. After all, he and I have a special connection. I know, I know, he's going out with my sister. But it's not a romantic connection I'm talking about; it's something different.

Benjamin knows me. And that knowledge, that bond, doesn't just stop when the relationship is over. I know him fairly well, too. You can't just forget all the things you've learned about someone, the way someone suddenly appears beautiful to you, or the way you suddenly understand what the world might be like from some other perspective.

I got the impression that Nina thought I'd do something outrageous when Benjamin got his sight back, that I'd go all out for him, that I'd try to bowl him over with how great I look after all these years. Okay, I put on some makeup and a nice outfit, but what was I supposed to do? Try to look as grungy as possible?

The truth is Benjamin has never cared how I look. After all, the two of us went out when he was blind,

and as often as he called me
beautiful, it never had anything to do
with my outer appearance.

And despite all the changes he's
been going through, I guess I'd like
to think that when Benjamin sees me,
he sees the real me.

Two

Lucas felt Zoey's eyes bore into him. "Are you sure you're okay?" she asked plaintively. She had found him pacing alone in the parking lot.

"Zo, for the one-thousandth time, I'm fine," he insisted, planting a quick kiss on her cheek to put her at ease. She smelled like a mixture of baby lotion and the perfume she always wore—like tea and flowers.

"You sure?" Zoey asked, her face flushed. Lucas nodded.

Zoey cast him another one of her meaningful stares. "Well, okay, then," she said finally, her voice brimming with trepidation. "I have to run over to the football field. They need me for the writing club group photo. Do you want to come?"

Lucas shook his head. He didn't need to tag along after his girlfriend. "Well, then, can I leave my stuff with you?" Zoey asked.

"Sure," Lucas answered as he accepted

Zoey's yearbook and her graduation cap and purse. He was relieved to be alone as he watched her make her way across the field, her graduation gown dragging in the dirt.

Lucas wandered over to the edge of the field, his feet sinking into the damp mud, his toes cramped in the too-small dress shoes he hadn't worn since some random cousin's wedding. He stood there for a while, just surveying the scene in front of him. Louise Kronenberger, a girl he recognized as a friend of Jake McRoyan's, swept past him. "Can you believe it's all over?" she cried. She walked away before he could compose an answer.

A couple of jock-type underclassmen ambled by, their big sneakers making wet clomping sounds in the mud. They were slapping each other on the back, and Lucas heard one say: "We're seniors now, dude. Next year, we rule."

Lucas could see his mom standing with Kate at the refreshment table. His mom was wearing her *special occasions* suit. It was white with gold buttons, and she stood there smiling, probably a little overheated, drinking punch and happily engrossed in conversation with Kate, Jake, and Jake's dad, Mr. McRoyan.

She's standing there like nothing's happened, Lucas thought as he shifted Zoey's stuff in his arms and watched his mother make cheery small talk. *She's standing there as if this morning hadn't happened. . . .*

Lucas replayed the scene in his head. He and Kate had been eating toast and cereal when Mrs. Cabral had come downstairs to inform Lucas that his dad would not be attending Lucas's graduation ceremony. When Lucas had asked why, Mrs. Cabral had said his dad was sick in bed. Lucas had scoffed at that. His dad was one of Chatham Island's gruffest, most toughened fishermen. He was always sick with coughs and flus. It didn't stop him from going to work every day.

Lucas dug his heels into the ground. He had the sudden urge to find Zoey. Part of him wanted to grab her and say, "Let's get out of here." He wanted to tell her about his dad; he wanted to hear her tell him everything would work out. But the other part of him knew he just couldn't say anything. She was surrounded by friends and family. How could he possibly explain to her that his own father didn't even care enough to show up at his graduation?

"Hey, Lucas!" Nina Geiger waved at him. She was sitting on a folding chair by herself, absently munching on a cookie, a full glass of punch in her hand, her Discman over her ears.

As Zoey's best friend and Benjamin's girlfriend, Nina was around the Passmore house all the time. Despite the fact they'd spent a lot of time together out of necessity, Lucas had never really gotten to know her. Maybe that was because he was always a bit wary of her. Nina was a little out of her mind—she was always dying her hair a different color and blasting her music loud enough to reach the mainland. And she had recently run away, leaving Chatham Island in the middle of the night. Lucas would have thought that had been cool had it not seemed so selfish. He'd been the one who'd had to console Zoey—she'd been totally brokenhearted.

Still Lucas found himself approaching Nina. A diversion was a diversion. "Hey," he said.

She turned down her Discman but barely looked up, still munching slowly on the chocolate chip cookie she'd been holding in her hand for the past few minutes.

"What's in there?" Lucas asked, pointing to the Discman.

"Listen." Nina pulled Lucas down by his tie. He choked a little. "It's the new No Doubt song." She put one headphone to his ear and the other to hers. "It sounds like Madonna but kind of ska," she added. "The lyrics are cool."

"It sounds like all they're saying is 'Don't speak' over and over again," Lucas answered.

"Yeah, words the principal and my yawn-a-thon valedictorian of a sister should live by," Nina droned.

"Claire's speech wasn't too bad," Lucas said, laughing.

"Um, can you say dysfunctional?" Nina barked. "I mean, the girl didn't thank anyone. Not me, not our dad. I mean, you'd think we actually liked living with her."

"Well, I don't know," Lucas said. "It wasn't the Oscars. . . ."

"Talk to the hand," Nina retorted, doing her best Ricki Lake imitation as she held out her flat palm to him. "I can't hear any Claire's-really-just-so-great talk. I get enough of it at home."

"Sorry." Lucas turned his attention to a group of girls from the cheerleading squad, including Melissa Kraus, who distinguished herself by being the hands-down perkiest girl on the squad. The girls broke into one of their old football cheers.

"Way to go, Krausketeer!" Nina called out.

Lucas watched as Nina brushed the

crumbs off her faded T-shirt. It was white with blue trim, and it had a picture of a Muppet on it, some fuzzy red one that looked like an alien. "Enough of this hoopla already," she grumbled.

"I'm right there with you," he agreed, surprised at the sudden kinship he felt with Nina. Maybe because as far as he was concerned, leaving Chatham Island for the University of Maine didn't count as a major life adventure. And Nina wasn't going anywhere, either—at least not this year.

Lucas looked up and saw Zoey and Benjamin trudging toward them across the field. Zoey had a disposable camera in her hand and a bunch of other graduates—Aisha Gray and Louise Kronenberger, among them—in tow. "I want a picture of you!" Zoey clamored, throwing her arms around Lucas, waving the camera around in her hand.

"Zoey, I need to take my mom home," Lucas whispered in her ear.

"It'll just be a second," Zoey pleaded, stroking his cheek with her palm. "Please . . ."

"One shot," Lucas responded, gazing down at her smiling face. She was so beautiful, so happy and innocent all at once. So different from him.

"Yeah," Nina muttered. "One shot, and

let's pretend like we're in one of those soda commercials having the best time of our lives. Where are the blond girls, the rope swings, and the cooler when you need them?"

The group lined up. "One . . . two . . . three!" Zoey called out. Everyone smiled. Lucas forced his face into what he hoped resembled a smile. "Excellent!" Zoey said, shooting him an imploring glance. "Can we just get one more?"

"You'll have to call my agency for that," Nina protested, walking out of the picture. "Tell them I'm difficult, I don't care. . . ."

Lucas smiled genuinely this time. *Whoever thought I'd be stoked to have Nina Geiger around,* he thought.

Claire Geiger stood against the brick wall near the field, trying to look as inconspicuous as possible.

"Congratulations, Claire!" called out a girl Claire knew she should recognize, but didn't.

"Thanks," Claire replied, smiling and doing her best to appear gracious.

"Will you sign my yearbook?" asked another girl, whose name Claire couldn't recall.

"Sure," Claire answered her. She took a pen out of her bag and hoped the girl didn't realize she was struggling to remember what class she knew her from.

Claire clutched her valedictorian award in one hand and did her best to set herself apart from the throng of graduates and their parents. She tried to appear occupied by burying her head in the Weymouth High School yearbook, but that didn't seem to stop the endless parade of people approaching her. Everybody wanted her yearbook signature, and in turn she had to ask them to sign hers.

Claire's classmates basically left the same signature in her book.

> *Dear Claire,*
> *I didn't really know you very well. You always seemed so distant. Good luck in your future. You're very smart.* (If the writer was a guy, he'd add: "and you're really pretty.") *Congratulations on getting into MIT and have a great life. See you in ten years at the reunion!*

Then whoever it was would scrawl his or her signature with his/her phone number. Sometimes, especially if the girl was a cheerleader type, there'd be a smiley face with "call me" written in big bubble letters. For a moment Claire wondered what her high-school years would have been like if she had allowed her classmates to be more a part of her life. Would she have been happier? Would she be a bit less lonely now?

Looking around at all the graduates as they hugged, cried, and took photos, Claire had the overwhelming sense that she should feel more than she was actually feeling.

The second the ceremony had ended, Nina had put her Discman on her head and planted herself on a lone chair in the middle of the field, looking to Claire like some bizarre surrealist painting. And her father was off giving his new wife, Sarah Mendel, a tour of the campus. That's how it had been ever since her father's wedding—he and Sarah immersing themselves in blissful isolation.

I should consider that a blessing, Claire reminded herself as she walked along the wall, her gaze fixed directly in front of her. After all, with their parents so preoccupied, it had been easy for her and Aaron Mendel, Sarah's son, to keep their romance a secret. Claire wondered if her dad was going to get concerned soon that she didn't have a boyfriend, when the truth was she had one.

Claire had kept meaning to tell her dad and

Sarah that she and Aaron were seeing each other, that they'd gone to her prom together, that since they were both going to be in Boston next year, their romance was going to continue.

Claire knew she owed it to her father to be as honest as possible. But she'd never found the right moment. Plus, how would her father react? Claire feared the worst. She could just hear her dad now: "Claire, I'm sorry, but dating Sarah's son is just not appropriate." And what if he tried to stop her from seeing Aaron? What would she do then?

The air was hot and heavy, and she used both hands to lift her thick black hair off the back of her neck. Maybe the whole thing was more trouble than it was worth, anyway. After all, Aaron hadn't even shown up for her graduation. What kind of boyfriend was he?

Almost as if he could hear her thoughts, he appeared by her side.

"What are you doing here?" she cried, suddenly breathless.

He touched her cheek softly, brushing the hair back from her face. "I had to congratulate you on being valedictorian," he said, a lock of blond hair falling into his face, his lips curled in a half smile. He held out a long-stemmed yellow rose. It was wrapped in purple tissue paper.

Claire took the rose and sniffed it, trying to hide her face momentarily as she looked down at the flower. She felt a blush rise to her forehead. "I can't believe you're here," she said. "I wasn't expecting you for a couple of days. I thought . . ." Her voice trailed off as she met his eyes and saw their warmth.

"I left early." Aaron pulled her closer. "I had a change of plans," he added enigmatically. He wrapped his arms around her shoulders, but Claire pulled away.

"Your mom's nearby," she whispered.

"Say no more," he said softly, dropping his arms. "But we're going to have to deal with this soon. I mean, we're about to have a lot of time together. I'm going to live at Chez Geiger for a few weeks."

"Aaron, you are?" Claire nestled her head on Aaron's shoulder. He put his arms around her again, and she kissed his neck and the bottom of his chin.

Out of the corner of her eye Claire saw fast approaching a slim figure in a light pink dress, a matching pocketbook slung over her elbow. "Your mom," Claire gasped. She jumped away from Aaron and tried to cool her flaming cheeks by waving her graduation program in front of her face.

"Aaron, darling, is that you?" Sarah Mendel called out, her pace quickening as she came closer.

"Mom," Aaron said, winking at Claire. "I've been looking for you!"

Nina

I was the first thing Benjamin Passmore saw when he got his sight back. He keeps saying how amazing that was.

Which just shows how far he'll go to make me feel good. I mean, if I'd known he was going to show up at the Malibu Hotel when I was there "in hiding," only to fall on the floor, writhe in pain, and regain his sight after a zillion years . . . well, I would have at least washed my hair. I would have even put fresh lipstick on.

But, of course, I didn't know. And what Benjamin got when his sight returned to him was a vision of full-on grunge-o-rama. And I don't mean that in some glamorous alt rock kinda way. I mean, stringy hair with roots for days, combination skin (I'm surprised he wasn't blinded by the oil slick that my nose had become!), unplucked brows . . . not to mention the fact that I'd been wearing the same clothes for days. Literally days.

You gotta feel sorry for the guy. I mean, if I were Benjamin, I'd much rather have the first

thing I saw be a beautiful sunrise,
or some amazing piece of art, or
the cast of 90210.

   I mean, anything would have been
better than the hagacious
wreckage that was me. And if
Benjamin can overlook the mother
of all disaster areas that was me
in the Malibu Hotel, I guess it
must really be true love.

Three

Lara McAvoy had a headache. And it wasn't just any headache. It was a megasize major whopper of a headache. If this wasn't a migraine, Lara didn't know what was: She felt as if she were going to die.

It didn't help that everything surrounding her was glaringly white: white walls, white sheets, white furniture, not to mention all the people coming in and out wearing white hospital coats. Even opening her eyes was painful.

What happened to me? Lara moaned. She was lying on an unfamiliar cot, in an unfamiliar room, in an unfamiliar outfit, holding her head in her hands, trying desperately to bring some semblance of order to the jumble of thoughts and memories in her head.

Think. Think hard, she whispered to herself, taking a deep, long breath. *It'll come to you.*

She lay there. *Something to do with a car,* she thought. *I was in the car, and then that*

awful Kate Levin was in another car, and
someone got into an accident, but was it me?
And then I was at the Passmores' house, and
everything was all torn up. But what did that
have to do with me? And then I was in a car
with my dad and he was telling me what a
mess I am, and now I'm here, and—

A stranger's voice interrupted her thoughts.

"Welcome to Serenity Hills, Lara. It's time
to wake up." It was a man's voice, and Lara
could detect a bit of an accent. Spanish or
something.

Lara opened her eyes to a squint. Her head
pounded. "Hi," she muttered.

"Hi," the man's voice said. The guy
sounded friendly enough. "My name is
Umberto, and I met you last night, although
you probably don't remember." Lara didn't respond. He paused. "Uh, you know, you were
pretty wrecked."

"I was?" Lara asked.

"Yes, you were," the man explained.
"You were with your dad, and you were
screaming about how you didn't want to be
here, and then you passed out right in the
lobby. You threw up on yourself first.
That's why you have different clothes on
this morning."

Lara lifted the white sheets off of her to

see that she was dressed in a T-shirt and sweatpants, both of which said Serenity Hills on them.

"We'd like to introduce you to the therapy group you'll be working with. Everyone's meeting in a half hour, Lara. You should probably try to get up," Umberto said. His tone was gentle but gruff.

"Wh-What is this place?" she stuttered.

"Wow, you really did black everything out from last night," Umberto said. "This is a re-habilitation center."

Rehabilitation? Lara thought incredulously. *Isn't that for like old people and cripples and stuff?* Lara pulled the white sheets up to her neck, but it didn't help her to feel any less vulnerable to the alien environment she found herself in.

"Lara," Umberto said firmly, "you have some substance abuse issues. You're here to detox. Get your life together. Your family was worried about you."

Yeah, right, Lara thought. *That's why I'm here. My family. They just wanted me out of their hair. They never exactly asked for me in the first place.*

"I look forward to seeing you in group in twenty minutes," Umberto said as he stood up to leave. "I'll send a nurse to come pick you up. Until then, I suggest you open your eyes all the way and acclimate yourself to your surroundings. You'll be surprised to find it's actually quite nice here. I know it's painful at first, but you have to feel worse before you feel better. That's just the way it goes. If you let yourself, you'll be very comfortable here, I'm sure." At that, he stood up and walked out.

Lara sat up in bed. It felt like a hammer was hitting her head at regular intervals. *I want a drink,* she thought. *A quick shot of vodka would take away the pain in my head.*

The room she was in was small and sparse. There was nothing on the wall—no art, nothing. There wasn't even a phone by the bed. There was a nightstand with a clock on it, though. And a little white machine that had a red button on it. There was a little label on the machine that said Nurse.

I'm in hell, Lara thought, flopping back down on the bed.

At that moment the door opened to reveal a woman in a nurse's uniform. She was a husky woman with blond curly hair and a lot of makeup. She reminded Lara of the tourists who came to the Passmores' restaurant, the fat ladies who always came for the early bird special. "Welcome, Lara," the woman said.

"Don't people knock around here?" Lara grumbled. "Or do they always just barge right in?"

"I'll be escorting you to meet the group, and then we'll set you up with an individual counselor," the woman replied, as if she didn't hear Lara. She walked toward the bed and peered down at Lara. "I promise, it won't be that bad. You might even find it fun."

A vodka martini is fun, Lara thought. *A hot toddy is fun. Meeting a group of drunks is not fun.*

The nurse stood above Lara. Lara saw no choice but to do as she was asked. She stood up, and a wave of nausea passed through her body. She leaned back against the bed, but the nurse grabbed her by the elbow. "The more you get up and move around, the better you'll feel," she instructed. Lara didn't say anything. She didn't bother to check what she looked like in the mirror or even to wash her face. She just slipped on a pair of white cotton slippers that were sitting next to the bed and followed the nurse out the door. "My name is Esmerelda," the nurse said.

And I'm Glinda, Lara thought.

Esmerelda led Lara into a big white room that was full of folding chairs. There were ten people sitting around, chatting. They were all dressed in sweats and T-shirts like Lara's. *A bunch of old freaks,* Lara thought. Each and every one of these people looked like they were in their thirties, at the very youngest. The women looked haggardly, and the men were potbellied, washed-up-looking guys, the kind whose advances Lara dodged when she went to the local bar.

There is no way I'm going to talk to these people, Lara thought, standing off to the side, surveying the scene.

"Group, I'd like you to say hello to our new member, Lara," Esmerelda began. "Lara, we understand you're probably going to feel a bit shy. Just open up whenever you're ready."

Lara looked down at the ground in silence. She could feel tears well up in her eyes. *Just don't cry in front of them,* Lara instructed herself. *Anything but cry.*

Esmerelda went around the group, asking each and every person how their day was. Once everyone spoke, Esmerelda addressed her. "Lara?" she said. "It wouldn't hurt for you to tell us a bit about yourself and how you got here."

"I—I . . . ," Lara stuttered. She could feel the silence of her companions as if it were a weight lying across her shoulders. Why was she here? She was here because her family didn't love her. Because she was the unwanted daughter. Because Zoey was the one they all loved. Because all her life no one had ever cared for her or treated her as though they considered her someone special.

There was no way Lara was going to share this with a roomful of strangers. There was no way she was going to endure the pity of a bunch of red-faced nutcases. *I've got to get out of here. I've got to.*

"Lara? Anything?" Esmerelda urged softly.

They're treating you like some lunatic; why not act like one? Lara thought. She looked up, opened her mouth, and began to scream. A train of epithets came pouring out of her mouth. "You losers!" she screamed. "Like I'm going to tell you anything about myself. You're just a bunch of idiots. My head hurts. Gimme some vodka . . . now. Bunch of gross old housewife drunks and fat booze-head bar hounds! I don't need any of you!"

At that Lara got out of her seat and surveyed the sea of gaping faces in front of her. *Maybe I can behave so awfully that they'll kick me out,* she thought. *Maybe I can get the hell out of here and get myself a drink.* She grabbed her chair, folded it up, and threw it to the ground. It made a huge crashing sound.

"That's it," Esmerelda said, standing up. She was calmer than Lara had expected her to be. "Umberto!" Esmerelda spoke into a walkie-talkie she kept in her nurse coat pocket. "We need some help down here."

Almost immediately Umberto strode into the room. "Back to your room, Lara," he said, staring her in the face.

Lara edged away. They wouldn't force her to go. They couldn't.

"Let's go, Lara," Umberto cajoled.

"No!" Lara barked. "Don't touch me."

Umberto pulled his walkie-talkie from his hospital coat. He pushed a red button, and four hospital orderlies walked in the door. "Want us to lift her up?" one of them asked.

Lara took one look at the group of very large men. *"This is abuse! I'm going to report you!"* she screamed, but the instant she saw the huge musclemen, she knew she'd lost. *At least I'm getting out of talking to those freaks,* she thought as two orderlies escorted her out, one on each arm. *And I'll just have to find some other way to get the hell out of here.*

Nina held Benjamin's hand as they made their way along the rocky beaches that lined Chatham Island. Nina had taken her shoes off, and she could feel the rocks, wet and mossy, under her feet as she walked.

"I never thought I'd see that lighthouse

again," Benjamin was saying, his voice momentarily wistful, as they stood on the rocks, the lighthouse gleaming on the water, the lights of North Harbor flashing in the background.

"Oh, Benjamin," Nina said, slipping her arm through his. She never really knew what to say when Benjamin made those kinds of revelatory statements, and these days he was making them quite often.

The two stood in silence for a minute, and Nina thought back over the past week. It had been quite an intense one.

When people asked Nina what she had done during the time she'd run away from home, she always gave the same answer: "Nothing, really." And basically she was telling the truth. During the two days that Nina had run away, she'd taken a couple of buses, hung out in a couple of skanky hotel rooms and bus stations, eaten fast food. And she'd almost been mugged or worse. She tried not to think about that part. But for the most part it had been pretty boring. She'd been too depressed to do much of anything except cry and eat and watch TV.

That is, of course, until Benjamin had come in search of her. It was funny the way things had worked out: Nina had run away because she'd caught Benjamin in a clinch with Kate. Of course, it had turned out that there was nothing between Kate and Benjamin, and now Kate was with Jake. But Nina hadn't known that at the time. She'd run away because she couldn't stand the thought of Benjamin with anyone else but her.

Yet somehow her running away had mobilized Benjamin into action, and he'd come and found her in Boston. Not that it had been that hard: She'd gone to the same hotel they'd stayed at last Valentine's Day. They both agreed that the Malibu Hotel, dump that it was, must have something special about it: After all, it was there that Benjamin had gotten his sight back. It had happened only minutes after they'd reunited.

And now they were back home. Benjamin had his sight back, they were a couple again, and the summer was in front of them.

Nina's T-shirt was sticking to her skin, and she had a momentary pang that maybe she was totally sweaty and smelly, but she decided to forget about it. After all, didn't communing with nature go together with grunge as smoothly as trail mix?

Nina tugged on the edge of Benjamin's T-shirt and pointed to a smooth rock by the water that looked big enough for both of them. "Wanna sit down?" she asked.

"No, let's keep walking," Benjamin said, clutching her hand. "I want to get a better look at the lighthouse."

Nina deferred to him, and they kept walking. The sun was setting, and Benjamin turned to her. "Have I told you how you look like a painting under this light?" he asked all of a sudden. Nina looked up at Benjamin's face beaming down at her. She still wasn't completely used to it without the trademark Ray-Ban sunglasses. He looked younger this way.

"Like a Modigliani," Benjamin said finally, cupping Nina's face in his hands. He held it, just staring at her for a few seconds.

Nina hadn't really paid attention to her evil art history professor, Mr. Buticelli, this year, and now she was regretting it. Since he'd gotten his sight back, Benjamin had been poring over all her art books from the class and saying things like, "I'm so happy to be able to be a true aesthete again."

"Your face is all hot," Benjamin whispered, reaching down to give Nina a gentle kiss on the lips.

That's because I'm embarrassed, Nina thought. Immature as it was, any mention of

Nina's looks made her feel a little amiss. Maybe it was just the newness of it all. Benjamin suddenly seemed so interested in her appearance and her prettiness (or lack thereof), as if her looks were a really important matter.

Nina felt suddenly self-conscious. *I should have at least brushed my hair,* she thought. *I should have worn makeup. I should have done something.*

They walked down the rocks and toward the water. "Look at the lighthouse," Benjamin said. "I love the way it looks yellow under the lights," he added, holding her hand. "And look at the way the seagulls are swooping down."

A week ago Nina would have made some comment about how it all looked like a cheesy postcard, and couldn't they go home and watch MTV, but she didn't feel like doing that today. Here was Benjamin seeing for the first time since he was fourteen years old, and Nina felt that in some ways she was experiencing it with him. She didn't want to be too sentimental about the whole thing, but she felt like maybe, in some way or another, she was seeing things for the first time, too.

Aisha

What does Benjamin see when he sees me? I don't think about my looks, so I don't see why Benjamin should. I look older, I guess. And my hair is longer. But other than that, I'm still the same old Eesh who used to bug him as a kid.

Except for the fact that I'm engaged. It's funny, but somehow I expected to look different once I was engaged. Like all of a sudden I'd look older, more mature, like a full-fledged adult.

No such luck. I'm still an immature geek. Which is, I

would imagine, what Benjamin sees when he sees me—a bookish girl who can't be bothered to make sure her clothes do anything but cover her body.

Truth be told, I don't care what Benjamin sees when he sees me.

That's not an insult or anything . . . I just can't be bothered to think about it.

Four

Aisha Gray woke up to the smell of coffee brewing and sausage cooking.

She was a deep sleeper, and it took her a couple of minutes to figure out what was going on. *Oh, that's right,* she reminded herself. *The Brunch.*

Aisha's parents had taken it upon themselves to organize a major brunch for the Sunday morning following graduation day. Supposedly it was to honor Aisha and all of her most recent accomplishments—graduation from high school, her admittance to Princeton, her engagement to Christopher.

Aisha was relieved to have graduation day behind her. Not only was she thrilled to be a high-school graduate, she was also thrilled to know that it was the last time she, Christopher, and David Barnes would be in the same place at the same time. David Barnes had been a total dating mistake, and now, well, she wouldn't have to deal with it anymore. She had a whole summer to get ready for college and spend time with the true love of her life . . . Christopher Shupe.

"Breakfast's ready! Breakfast's ready!" Aisha's younger brother, Kalif, screamed. *Two decibels louder, and he's going to break my eardrums!* Aisha thought begrudgingly as she pulled herself out of bed.

By the time she made it downstairs, everybody was sitting around a table bedecked with breakfast goods. It was a gorgeous spread of biscuits, bagels, pancakes, eggs, and all different muffins, and Aisha felt her stomach groan with hunger.

Christopher stood up the minute she walked in the room. He was in dressed in his please-the-parents finest, his white oxford shirt tucked into khaki pants. "Hey, babe," he said, giving her a quick kiss on the cheek. She blushed. Her entire family was watching them.

"Ewwww, gross!" Kalif screamed.

"Grow up, Kalif," Aisha scolded, emerging from her embrace and taking a seat at the table between her mother and Christopher.

"You'll learn soon enough, little man," Christopher said, patting Kalif on the head and sitting down again.

It had probably taken the cooks at the inn

a few hours to prepare the brunch, but it took the Gray party all of a few minutes to consume it. By the time they'd gobbled up the food and Mr. Gray had completed what seemed like an endless series of mimosa toasts (they were very diluted), Aisha was so full, she felt sick.

"Would it be okay if Christopher and I took a walk?" she asked her parents.

"Of course, Eesh, honey," her mom said, planting a kiss on each of her daughter's cheeks. "We're so proud of you."

Wow. How long's this going to last? Aisha wondered. Usually her parents weren't really indulgent.

Aisha took advantage of the one time she wouldn't have to help clean up and scurried out of the inn, her hand in Christopher's. "Thanks, Mr. and Mrs. Gray," the ever polite Christopher called out.

"You're welcome, dear," Mrs. Gray responded pleasantly.

"Let's walk toward my apartment," Christopher said. "I gotta get ready for work soon."

"Okay," Aisha consented. "How long are you working, anyway?"

"I'm on a double shift today, Eesh. Lunch and dinner," Christopher answered.

"Oh, so I'm not going to see you until to-morrow," Aisha said, trying not to make her voice sound too guilt imposing.

"What will we do?" Christopher exclaimed melodramatically.

"Oh, shut up." Aisha laughed. "It's not like I don't have things to do myself. I have to go through all those course catalogs before I register for summer school tomorrow."

"Who'd have thought I'd end up marrying such a brain," Christopher said, chuckling.

"Pffft," Aisha grumbled, sticking out her tongue. "It's not like I was awarded valedictorian or anything."

"You'll always be valedictorian to me," Christopher said, wrapping his arms around her shoulders as they walked. Aisha laughed again. Thank God, none of her friends could hear how sappy she and Christopher were when they were alone. She could just see Nina Geiger sticking her finger down her throat, pretending to barf.

"You know," Christopher said, "high school just ended for you, but I feel like everything's just beginning for us."

"I know what you mean," Aisha said softly, thinking back to all the dreams she'd had recently—of her and Christopher and their life together.

As if Christopher could read her mind, he said, "Someday we'll live in a beautiful house right on the water, and you'll be a famous professor somewhere, and I'll build you a beautiful office with a view of the water, and I'll have some amazing business, and you'll go on trips with me all over the world."

"Oh, Christopher." Aisha sighed. "It's all so far away."

Images of a beautiful house, Christopher, dogs, and kids flooded her head as they approached the apartment complex. Aisha had concocted an amazing fantasy involving Nina and Zoey coming to visit, and all of them barbecuing on the beach in front of Christopher and Aisha's house, when she heard an unfamiliar voice call Christopher's name: "Christopher Shupe, I've been waiting for you for so long."

Aisha's vision focused to the stoop in front of Christopher's building, where a long-legged girl sat. She was reading a book and resting her feet on a huge valise in front of her. As far as Aisha could tell, she was beautiful—she had smooth, olive-toned chocolate brown skin, long curly hair, and what looked like an amazing body. She was, perhaps, the most beautiful girl Aisha had ever seen who was still a teenager and wasn't in a fashion magazine.

Aisha looked up at Christopher. "Who is that?" she asked. She was totally confused. Christopher hadn't said anything about having visitors, certainly not one who was remotely her age, a girl, and a total babe!

"Oh, my God," Christopher let out, dropping his arm from around Aisha's back and just standing there, a dumbfounded look on his face. "Eesh," he said abruptly, "I'll call you later. You should go."

"I should *what?*" Aisha stammered incredulously. She had been planning on going up to Christopher's apartment with him, maybe kissing him for a while, and then walking him to work. She hadn't expected to leave him standing in front of his apartment with a beautiful girl and her luggage.

"Eesh, I'm serious—I'll explain later," Christopher stuttered. They had stopped walking and were just standing there, not ten feet away from his apartment.

"I'm so happy to see you," the girl cried as she stood up. She was wearing a little pink T-shirt and a long black skirt and black flip-flops. She stood on the stoop expectantly.

"Eesh, can I come over later?" Christopher said, his gaze directed straight at the girl. "I'll explain everything. I'll . . ."

"I guess so," Aisha answered. *Don't you*

want to introduce me to your friend? her mind was screaming. But the words weren't coming to her. She felt a cold wave of apprehension settle over her as she walked away.

"Okay, Jake, so you gotta make sure that the meat is firmly packed, like so," Max said, holding a raw hamburger patty in his big red hand and tossing it onto the oily grill.

"Got it," Jake replied.

Jake was wearing the full Burger Heaven regalia—a T-shirt, baseball cap, apron, and jeans. Jake and his teammates always went to Burger Heaven for a burger and fries after their games. It was funny to be clad in the outfit he'd watched so many people wear over the years. Burger Heaven was a Chatham Island staple. Especially for athletes.

It was on Dock Street, near the ferry landing, and it was also huge with tourists, whose idea of touring Chatham Island was getting off the boat, looking at the water, having something to eat, and getting back on the boat. Burger Heaven was always crowded.

As far as Jake could tell, his boss, Max, had two different moods: annoyed and more annoyed. He'd put Jake through the ringer this morning. After Jake had spent the morning memorizing the menu to learn how much everything cost, Max had tested him with a series of rapid-fire questions, like, "And what if I added extra lettuce and a side of mayo to that order—how much would it be then?" Finally he'd gotten to the real work—which was seasoning the meat, toasting the buns, mixing the special sauce, and grilling the hamburgers according to the customer's preference. Jake didn't know how he was ever going to get the smell of hamburger and onions off his hands.

"Jake, I gotta tell you," Max said as he tossed a couple of onions on the skillet. "I don't usually hire the high-school kids. They're a flighty bunch, you know."

"I just graduated, Max," Jake reminded him.

"Well, yeah," Max said gruffly. "My point is I try to stay away from the help that's not going to give me one hundred percent. But you seem like a good solid kid."

"Thanks—" Jake began.

"But let's get this straight, kid," Max interrupted. "I don't tolerate slacking. Not one bit."

"I understand, sir," Jake replied. *God, it's like Coach McNair all over again,* he thought. Jake was hoping to save up enough money to buy a car. He figured he'd need one next year at the University of Massachusetts. First of all, he knew he'd probably want to go into

Boston a lot, and second of all, he'd need it when Kate came to visit. They had already talked about spending weekends together next year when he was away.

"Okay, kid," Max instructed, "you gotta make sure the oil's real hot before you put the fries in, and then once you have the fries in, you gotta make sure you cook 'em for exactly two and a half minutes. Any less time, they're soggy. Any more time, they're too crispy. My customers expect them to be just so."

"Okay," Jake said, holding the wire basket of fries in front of him. "Should I do it now?" he asked.

"Yeah, right now. The oil's just hot enough," Max snapped. "Just make sure you put 'em in slowly, and hold on to the handle the whole time—otherwise you got oil spraying up everywhere, and the fries end up being a big greasy mess."

Jake realized that Max had actually succeeded in making him nervous about a vat of french fries. He could feel his boss's eyes boring into him. Just as the fries were about to hit the oil, he heard someone say, "Hi, I was wondering if Jake McRoyan is here?" It was Kate.

With the sound of Kate's voice Jake's stomach turned over a couple of times, and he had a momentary pang of regret that he'd told her to come visit him at work. *I must look like a total dork, dressed like this. I'm going to turn around, and she's going to be, like: Who the hell is this loser?*

"Yeah, he's here," Max replied gruffly. "But as you can see, he's busy. Come back later!"

At the thought of Kate's leaving without his even making eye contact with her, Jake panicked. He forgot all about the fries for a second and turned around to face her. To say she looked gorgeous would be the understatement of the millennium. Her hair was down and flowing, and it looked especially red against the black polo shirt she was wearing. Jake's eyes rested on her smiling face for a second and then traveled down her body. She was wearing cutoff jean shorts, and Jake loved the way her legs looked. Not too skinny, but perfectly sculpted.

"Kid, kid, watch what you're doing!" Max scolded harshly. Jake turned around to see that somehow—in the couple of seconds he'd turned away—he'd lost control of the wire basket of fries, which had plummeted to the bottom of the oily vat.

"Sorry," Jake mumbled. "I'm really sorry."

"Maybe it's time we discuss my policy about visitors," Max scoffed.

JAKE

Man, the last time Benjamin
saw me I was a little twerp,
a little wimp, an eleven-year-old
geekazoid who was coming over
to his house all the time to
hang out with his sister.

And now . . . well, I've grown.
I'm arguably the best athlete
in the school. Though I doubt
that Benjamin would really take
much notice of that.

I guess I probably look
pretty normal. Just your
average high-school jock. I don't
think that you can see by
looking at me that I nearly got

thrown off the football team for doing coke during a game. Or that I nearly threw away my life to alcoholism. Sometimes at my A.A. meetings someone will tell a story about some incredible ordeal they've been through, and I'm amazed because you'd never know it to look at them. Of course, some people's faces do look like they've been through hell. I hope mine doesn't.

Overall, I definitely think people underestimate "normal" as a way of being. I'd like to think that when Benjamin sees me, he just sees a normal guy.

Five

Zoey sat on the floor of her room, amid a sea of cards and envelopes, her yearbook open to the senior class address list.

Okay, she thought, *is it too over the top to write: You are invited to the graduation party of all graduation parties?*

Zoey leaned against the side of her bed and nibbled on the purple felt-tip pen she was using to compose. *It's times like this you really need Martha Stewart,* she realized as she reached for the phone. A second opinion was of the utmost necessity.

"Hello," Lucas answered.

"Hey," Zoey said. "I didn't wake you, did I?"

"No, I've been up for a while." Zoey knew Lucas well enough to know when he was unusually tense.

"Are you okay, babe?" she asked.

"I'm fine, Zo," Lucas answered.

This is very déjà vu, Zoey thought, her memory hearkening back to yesterday morning's graduation ceremony, when she'd repeatedly asked a very sullen Lucas what the problem was, and he'd repeatedly said, "Nothing."

"Oh, well, I was just going to bother you with a dumb question." Zoey suddenly felt unsure of herself. With Lucas in such a bad mood, she didn't want to say the wrong thing. *Don't mention California,* she thought. *Don't mention anything about college or next year or anything.*

"About what?" Lucas asked.

"The graduation party," Zoey replied. "Um, you know, I'm doing the invitations right now. I'm going to hand deliver them later."

"Oh," Lucas said. "I guess I kinda forgot."

Forgot? Zoey thought. *I've only been talking about the graduation party for days now.*

"Lucas, are you sure you're okay?"

"Yes," Lucas said. He paused. "And you have to stop asking me that."

"I know, I know," Zoey said. She felt strangely choked up, as if something very bad was about to happen. She had never heard Lucas sound so distant, so cut off. "I know it's annoying for me to keep asking you," she heard herself continue. "It's just that you seem so, I don't know, not yourself. . . ." Now that she'd started, Zoey felt the words tumbling from her mouth. "Do you want to come over or anything? We could deliver the invites together. Or just sit and talk for a while."

"I can't, Zo, I'm sorry," Lucas said in the same monotone. "I have stuff to do. I have to look for a job."

"Look, Lucas, if there's something wrong, I wish you would tell me what it is."

"Zoey." He said it softly, tenderly.

"Lucas, what is it?" Zoey urged.

"I just feel like—" But Lucas stopped abruptly.

Zoey could hear his father's voice calling to him gruffly.

"I'll talk to you later, Zoey. I have to go. Okay?" Lucas asked.

"Okay." Zoey listened to the click as Lucas hung up the phone. She wished she didn't feel this way when things went wrong with Lucas. As though she'd have to hold her breath until she spoke to him again. Until she understood. Until she knew for sure that everything was all right.

With morning sunlight easing its way through his open bedroom window and Rachmaninoff's Prelude in C-sharp Minor blaring from the CD player, Benjamin had the atmosphere perfectly set for the cleansing ritual he was about to perform.

Here we go, Benjamin thought as he opened the top drawer to his dresser. Inside were two stacks of gleaming white T-shirts staring up at him. They were starched and pressed, and folded symmetrically. He lifted one up and held it to his face: It was soft from overwashing, and it smelled like the fabric softener his mom used.

Now is the time, now is the hour, he thought, laughing at himself and the drama he was conjuring up alone in his room. He took the T-shirt and threw it in the wastebasket. It looked strange—a piece of cloth crumpled meaninglessly in the bottom of the wicker trash can. He quickly filled the basket with the rest of the shirts, ceremoniously disposing of them one by one.

If anyone saw me, they'd think I was crazy, Benjamin thought. *Or at least a vigilant anti-environmentalist.*

Benjamin walked across the room. On the floor next to the bed were five cardboard boxes. They were all open and brimming with clothes Benjamin had recently bought.

Benjamin pulled a pile of shirts out of a box. They were a medley of different colors and patterns. There were striped T-shirts, checkered button-downs, pullovers in greens, blues, and reds. He stacked them neatly and put them in the open drawer.

Ever since he'd been fourteen, when he'd woken up from illness to find himself in a dark world, in a world where your sight could suddenly be seized from you, he'd worn two colors: black and white. He'd forsaken patterns, stripes, colors, anything that required others to help him get dressed.

And now that he could see, those days were over. He would forget that they had ever existed.

Benjamin opened his bottom drawer. It was crammed tight with pair after pair of worn-out black jeans. He leaned down, flattening the pile with his hand, then straightened when he heard a knock on the door. He knew it was Nina.

"Hey," he called out. Rachmaninoff was still blaring, but it was a more romantic and less dramatic piece now, "Rhapsody on a Theme," played by Paganini. Benjamin felt for a second like they were in a movie and the sound track was shifting to let the audience know they were in store for a little romance.

"Hey," Nina said. She had two steaming foam cups in her hands. "I brought you some coffee," she said, handing him one.

"Thanks." He took the cup from her and placed it carefully on the nightstand. He glanced at Nina and smiled. She was wearing a pair of cutoff dark khaki shorts and an old red-and-white I Love New York T-shirt her father had brought her from one of his business trips. Her dark hair was loose, and she pushed it impatiently behind her ears when it swung into her face.

Benjamin took her hand and led her toward the bed. She had seemed tense when she first entered the room, but the minute he touched her, she seemed to relax. "Is this your idea of how to tip the delivery girl?" she asked.

He laughed and kissed her lightly on the mouth. Her lips tasted sweet, like sugar and milk.

"What were you doing when I got here?" Nina asked, her eyes focusing in on the trash can, which overflowed with T-shirts.

"A little spring cleaning," Benjamin answered, nuzzling his face in the crook of Nina's soft neck. "You know, before I start the day. . . ."

"Speaking of the day," Nina murmured, "I was wondering if we could, you know, hang out together."

Benjamin looked at her. She looked so earnest all of a sudden. "Cool," he said.

Nina looked up at him, her eyes wide and round. "I was kind of thinking," she stumbled. "Remember when I used to come here and read to you?"

"Aw, Nina," Benjamin replied, squeezing her tighter. "Of course I do."

"I was thinking," Nina said, "that we could do that again today . . . that we could, you know, just hang out here . . . like old times. I could even read to you. And then you could read to me. . . ."

What is she talking abut? Benjamin thought. *Why would I want to hang out here, in my room, doing things I used to do when I was blind? What would be the point of that?* He knew he'd have to put what he was about to say delicately.

"You know, I have to tell you, Nina," he said, his hands caressing her shoulders, "there's nothing more I love than being with you, but I feel like I've been trapped in this room since I was fourteen. The last thing I want to do is, you know, spend another day here."

"Yeah, kind of stupid of me." Nina laughed. "I guess that's like asking someone who just got back his hearing if he wants to watch Marlee Matlin translate a John Tesh concert into sign language, or like asking a hostage who just got released if he wants to go to a vegan restaurant for dinner, or like . . ." Her voice trailed off before she could complete her signature three-part joke.

"Nina, it wasn't stupid of you," Benjamin said. "It's just that it's summer and I have two months until college. I don't want to sound too much like a TV movie, but I just want to fit in as much as I can."

"The Benjamin Passmore story," Nina quipped.

"Nina, I want to start doing different things," Benjamin continued. "I've been in the dark for so long. I want to be outside, seeing things, seeing everything. I want to explore, you know. Do everything I haven't been able to do for so long."

Benjamin knew what she was wondering: *Does that include me?* And of course, it did. Nina was the most important thing in the world to him.

"I know you're going to think this is crazy, but, well . . ." *Just get it out,* he instructed himself. "Well, I've always wanted to learn to surf."

"Excuse me," Nina said. She looked aghast. Benjamin could see she was trying to suppress a laugh, and he told himself not to feel hurt by that. It *did* sound somewhat absurd. "Surfing?" she said incredulously. "You want to try surfing? Like the Beach Boys?" She tittered.

"Yes," Benjamin said. This time he wouldn't indulge her by laughing at himself.

Nina grabbed her coffee off the nightstand

and took a sip. He could tell she was trying to occupy herself because she didn't know what else to do.

For a moment they were completely silent.

"You know, you could learn, too. You might like it," Benjamin said.

"I don't think so." Nina swallowed. "But I guess I could just watch," she added. "Maybe you'll get really good. That would be so cool."

Benjamin was touched. He knew that it took a monumental effort for Nina to swallow her sarcasm. "Just as long as you're there with me," he said, "I can't go wrong."

LUCAS

When Benjamin looks at me,
he's looking at his sister's
boyfriend, so he's probably
kind of critical. I mean,
I'm sure he expects the
best for Zoey.

I guess I don't look
like a loser or anything.
People say I'm handsome
and stuff, but let me
tell you, I've also heard
that you look how you feel.

I wonder if Benjamin
looks at me and sees what
I see when I look in the
mirror. A guy who's been in

Youth Authority, which is practically jail. A guy who's headed for the University of Maine, while he and his sister and all their friends go to prestigious, Ivy League schools. A guy with no plans, no future.

Zoey would say I was being too hard on myself, but that's because she loves me.

And what happens if she finally clues in to the truth? What if one day we're sitting there, hanging out in her room, doing what we always do—just

being together And stuff,
And she looks At me And
finally notices thAt I
don't belong in her world?
I would do Almost Anything
to keep thAt from
hAppening.

Six

Lucas, your father wants to see you. Lucas, your father wants to see you. Lucas, your father wants to see you. . . .

Those were the first words out of his mother's mouth when Lucas came down to the kitchen for breakfast. Her mouth looked grim and her eyes were brimming with tears, so Lucas knew he was really in for it. *He misses my graduation. He screws up,* Lucas thought bitterly. *So now he has to put the blame on me.*

Lucas stood outside the door to his parents' bedroom for a moment before going in. *Probably a lecture on how I have to get a summer job, about how lazy I am,* he thought. *Of course he's not going to apologize for not having come to graduation. He's probably been out all morning on the boat, not even remembering that he ditched the ceremony yesterday.*

He felt a million things all at once. He wanted to open the door and scream at his father. *How could you not come to my gradua-tion? How could you let me down like that? How could you not care one bit?* But, of course, his father was a man with very little tolerance for emotional outbursts. As far as Lucas could tell, his father's life consisted of two things: work and talking about work. A whining son was the last thing he'd want to deal with.

Lucas opened the door to his parents' bed-room. It was pitch black inside. Lucas fum-bled around, unsure of himself at first. He couldn't even distinguish the bed from the nightstand.

"Lucas," his dad moaned. Lucas took a seat in the armchair next to the bed.

"Dad, I . . . uh . . . Mom said you wanted to see me," Lucas stammered. His eyes had ad-justed to the light, and he focused in on his dad lying under the covers of his bed. He was shocked at what he saw. His dad's face was a sallow yellow; his eyes, all puffy and red; his back, propped up by a mound of pillows.

"Lucas, I need to talk to you," his father whispered.

"Okay." Lucas tried to make his voice sound relaxed so his father couldn't tell how scared he was.

"I haven't been feeling well." His father

groaned. "I had the flu yesterday, and today when I went to get up, I threw my back out."

"I'm—I'm sorry, Dad. That's really rough," Lucas said.

Way to say the obvious, he thought angrily.

His father coughed and took a sip of water from a glass on the nightstand. He cleared his throat. "Lucas, I've called you in here to talk about your summer employment."

"I—I—I've been meaning to talk to you about that, too," Lucas stammered. Leave it to his dad to be flat out on his back and still worrying whether Lucas was going to pull his weight around the house. "I was going to go job hunting today, actually."

There was silence for a moment. "Lucas," his father said at last, "I'm afraid you're going to be working on the boat this summer."

Lucas dug his hands into the arms of the chair. He could feel his head start to throb and his throat start to clog. It was like he was going to explode. *I should have known.* Lucas groaned inwardly. *I should have known that's what he was going to say. Of course.*

"Lucas," his father continued, "the doctor says I have to stay off my feet for at least six weeks. I'd be the first person to tell you that this guy doesn't know his head from his elbow, but you know your mother. . . ."

Lucas searched desperately for something to say. "What about the other fishermen?" he asked. He knew he was grasping at straws. "I'm sure they could do it."

"No, son." His dad's tone was gruff and stern; his answer, automatic. "I'm not letting this boat out of the family. There's no question."

His dad was in lecture mode now. "This is prime lobster season," he continued. "We're losing valuable time and money every minute that boat's not in use."

As his father spoke—about family heritage, about honor and respect—one thing became perfectly clear to Lucas: His future, at least for the next six or so weeks, was settled. Starting at dawn every morning he'd be on that boat, catching lobsters.

That's what his summer was going to be. Zoey would be throwing graduation parties. He'd be degutting lobsters.

I'm afraid you'll be working on the boat this summer, his father's voice echoed through his head. Lucas couldn't remember ever before hearing a word of regret from his father's mouth in regard to his expectations and demands for Lucas. *He must be really sick,* Lucas realized with a sudden pang. *But even when he's trying to be nice, he screws me over.*

*   *   *

Nina peered above the rims of the cheap tortoiseshell sunglasses she'd bought at the local drugstore.

Happy-go-lucky would be the last phrase in the world Nina Geiger would ever use to describe her boyfriend, but watching Benjamin teeter about on the edge of his brand-new surfboard—his dark hair whipping in the wind, a look of vacant pleasure plastered on his face—made her wonder if the Benjamin she'd once known and loved had been replaced by some alien being.

"This is just the most bizarre thing I've ever seen," Nina moaned. She was curled up on a giant Coca-Cola towel facing the water, picking at a scab she had on her elbow and sipping a mango-lemonade Snapple.

"Nina, don't be overdramatic," Aisha snapped. She was sitting on the sand, a text-book in front of her. Nina didn't even bother to ask what the book was about. Aisha was always reading some obscure tome, even when they didn't have school.

"Yeah, Nina, get a grip," Zoey added. "You act like this is that show *Road Rules* and Benjamin's about to bungee jump into a volcano or something crazy. He's just surfing."

"Okay, okay," Nina griped, "maybe I'm overreacting. Maybe watching your boyfriend turn into a beach blanket bimbo before your very eyes is a completely normal thing." She pulled out her trademark pack of Lucky Strikes from her backpack. *This will calm me down,* she thought. She removed a cigarette, packed it down on the palm of her hand, and gingerly placed it between her lips. She sucked in, as if she were taking the biggest drag of smoke in her life. Of course, she'd neglected to light the thing. That was how Nina kept her habit healthy—not lighting the cigarette was one way never to inhale.

Nina wanted to appear as accepting as possible of Benjamin's new hobby, mind-boggling as it was. She'd even managed an "Oh, cool!" when Benjamin showed her the new wet suit and board he'd ordered. "We should get you one, too!" he'd exclaimed, but Nina had demurred. The thought was just too ghastly. *Could anything be more absurd than me in a wet suit?* she thought. *That's kind of like when you order sushi, but you get the most fattening kind. It's like wrapping black seaweed around fatty tuna. I mean, my pale, chubby thighs surrounded by black rubber.*

A troop of bikini-clad girls, surfboards in hand, made it down to the edge of the water. They were all giggling, and one of them was humming a Hootie & the Blowfish song.

"Ew, hotties singing Hootie," Nina said. She paused for thought and pushed her glasses farther down her nose. "Hey, you guys, you don't think that maybe that's why Benjamin chose surfing . . . because he wanted to be near the babeage."

"Could you pick a more derogatory word?" Aisha muttered, turning the page of her book and not looking up.

"Okay," Nina replied defensively. "I take back *babeage*. How about this: Do you think Benjamin chose surfing because he wanted to be near more women-who-I'm-sure-are-very-intelligent-despite-the-fact-that-they-opt-to-wear-butt-floss?"

Aisha rolled her eyes, and Zoey—who was lying a towel over from Nina, reading a magazine—groaned. "Don't be absurd, Nina," she said, digging her hand in the sand and scooping up a clump. "Surfing has nothing to do with babeage or butt floss. Benjamin doesn't care about either of those things. Just because he can see again doesn't mean he's going to have an entirely new set of values. He's still Benjamin."

Nina kept her eyes peeled on the girls walking toward the shore. As they traipsed down the beach in all their firm, muscular glory, she placed her hands on the tops of her legs. They felt mushier than usual. *Full-on oatmeal thighs*, she thought disgustedly.

Nina's eyes were drawn to a particularly fit girl in a royal blue halter top and pink bikini bottom. She was floating on a yellow surfboard, having situated herself next to Benjamin in the water. She was teaching him how to mount the board. "I'm sorry, but will you guys look at that girl?" Nina gasped longingly.

"What about her?" Zoey said. "She seems helpful, if that's what you mean."

"I'm talking about her body." Nina moaned. "It's so . . . so perfect."

"Well," Aisha said, as usual sounding ever rational, "it looks like she works out. Surfing probably burns a lot of calories. Plus body fat."

Nina couldn't take her eyes off the girl's taut body, her muscular arms, her perfectly sculpted legs, and she felt a pang in her stomach. "How come I have the sudden urge to eat a mountain of french fries?" Nina grumbled, standing up and putting a sweatshirt on over the T-shirt she was already wearing. "How many calories will I burn walking to the hot dog stand?" she asked.

"It doesn't work that way, Nina." Zoey laughed. "But I'll come with you if you're going to get stuff. I want to use the pay phone to call Lucas."

"Hey, where is Lucas?" Aisha asked.

"At home," Zoey answered, slipping her

feet into flip-flops. "I don't know—he was really weird on the phone today."

"Come on," Nina said. "If I have to watch these *Baywatch* rejects for another second, I think I'll lose my mind. And I'd like to scarf down a jumbo order of curly fries while I still have all my capacities intact!"

Seven

Claire stood atop the widow's walk that lay outside her room, the breeze from Lighthouse Road brushing against her face. She combed her fingers through her wet hair. She knew she should probably go downstairs and blow it dry before it started to frizz, but the air was so still and gentle, and the sound of the breeze so peaceful.

Claire had taken the Sunday morning after graduation (and most of the afternoon) to sleep in. It was her prerogative, she figured. She'd lain in her air-conditioned room, beneath cotton sheets and an antique quilt that used to belong to her mother, and listened as the rest of the household had risen and gone about their days. Her dad had gone off to church, she figured, and Nina had probably gone off with Benjamin. Where the Mendels had gone, she wasn't sure, but she imagined Sarah had taken Aaron shopping, maybe.

These days having the Geiger household to

one's own for even an hour was a rare treat, and Claire had been sure to take advantage of it. She'd done a full beauty treatment: She'd showered, done a deep condition on her hair, shaved her legs, and done two facial masks—one to cleanse, the other to hydrate. She'd even given herself a manicure—she'd used clear polish, of course, not black like that psycho sister of hers.

The widow's walk above her room was Claire's favorite place on earth; she always felt comfortable there—to think, study, stare into the sky and examine the weather phenomena. She wondered if she'd find somewhere like it at MIT. *Probably I'll just be in labs all day,* she thought. *I'll be studying the weather without actually looking at it.* There was never again going to be a place like the widow's walk: so much light, such a good view, and it was away from everything and everybody.

"Hey, Claire, you up there?" The sound of Aaron Mendel's voice caught her off guard.

She peered down the ladder. "Aaron, I'll be right there," she called down.

"Don't bother! I'm coming up," he yelled back.

"Aaron, don't!" Claire cried, but it was too late. She peered down the ladder entry to see Aaron Mendel's head bobbing up and down as he climbed toward her. In a rush of modesty Claire shook out her hair and tied her robe tighter. She usually liked to be in control of how she appeared to others, and Aaron's habit of bursting in on her made that difficult.

"Whoa," he said when he poked his head up. "It's high up here."

"Aaron, haven't you heard of privacy!" Claire scolded.

"I'm sorry," Aaron murmured, though Claire could hear from the coyness in his tone that he didn't mean it even remotely. "Do you want me to leave?"

Claire knew she should say yes. Claire knew she should send him back down, rebuff him; but he looked so cute in his jeans and white T-shirt, his blond hair in need of a haircut. "Is this what you plan on doing instead of summer school?" Claire taunted him. "Invade my personal space?"

Aaron chuckled. "Well, at least for a good few weeks."

"A few weeks," Claire repeated. "Right. Well, might now be an appropriate time to ask what your mysterious summer plans are?"

"Yeah, I guess you should know," Aaron answered. "We're going on the road."

"We?" Claire asked indignantly. *We? Does he mean me and him? Excuse me, but I'm usually consulted on huge life plans*. Claire scowled. "Aaron," she reprimanded, "I hate to inform you, but I have a million things to do this summer."

"I'm sure you do," Aaron said, taking a deep breath. "But I'm talking about me and my band."

"Oh." Claire felt a blush creeping into her cheeks, but she decided to ignore it. She twirled a bit of hair in her hand and cast her gaze into the distance.

"We've got a little tour lined up," Aaron said. "You know, at different blues clubs across the country."

They stood quietly for a moment.

"Claire, you're not mad, are you?" Aaron asked, tossing a tousle of hair out of his eyes.

"No," Claire said. "Just a little surprised. Last time we talked, you didn't even mention this."

"Oh, well, it's kind of a spur-of-the-moment thing," Aaron responded. "We're going to Chicago and Detroit and then to New York. You should come and see us there!"

"Maybe," Claire said. She wasn't about to give Aaron that much. After all, she was still feeling a little embarrassed about her faux pas. She should have known he'd been referring to Wicked Undertow, the blues band his friends started at boarding school.

"You look beautiful with your hair all wet like that." Aaron finally broke the silence that had suddenly overcome them.

"I've got to go blow-dry it."

"You can do that in a second," Aaron replied. He hoisted himself up onto the walk and reached out to caress her face. He had the most beautiful eyes, the most flawless skin.

Aaron held the back of Claire's neck the whole time and, leaning closer, touched her lips tenderly with his own.

"You seem tense, Claire. Do you want a back rub?" he asked. "I always give good back rubs."

"Let's go down to my room," Claire murmured breathlessly. Her pulse was racing, and her heart felt as though it were going to take off.

They climbed down to her room and immediately jumped on her bed. Claire threw her arms around his neck and began trailing kisses from the corner of his mouth down toward his neck. She could hear muffled voices on the stairway, but she tried to block them out.

Then she heard another sound, a scraping, as if someone were turning her doorknob. Not even Nina would be so bold as to just enter her room without knocking. But suddenly the door swung open.

Claire leaped away from Aaron and sat bolt upright on her bed, trying to calm her breathing.

"Claire," her father poked his head in. "I was wondering if you wanted to grab some lunch."

"Hold on a sec," Claire said, her voice coming out strange and shrill. "I'll be right down."

"Right-o, Claire," they heard her dad answer. "I'll be waiting. Oh, and do you know where Aaron is? Sarah's looking for him."

"Nope." Claire put a hand over Aaron's mouth to silence him. He was shaking with laughter.

Christopher Shupe was reeling. *What in the world is she doing here? How could she just show up? It's not like my life isn't complicated enough; now I have to deal with this?*

He began to pace. It was a habit he'd picked up in the army barracks. There'd been nothing to do there in the off hours, especially when the gym and the canteen were closed. Now Christopher had the width of his apartment over which to stride. It wasn't very big, and it didn't take much time to make it from one side to the next.

She's getting on the next bus home. No question about it, he determined. *She's outta here. I have work to do. I have Aisha. I don't have time for this.*

Christopher felt as though his brains were about to explode. It had been a total head trip: walking with Aisha, holding her hand, thinking and talking about the future, feeling finally like things were good between them, settled. Only to be confronted with that figure on the stoop, with his past.

Christopher stopped midpace and inhaled. She was standing before him, the object of his anxiety—his sister, Kendra.

Christopher tried not to scrutinize her, but it'd been so long since he'd last seen her. Here in front of him was a young woman, an adult. *She must be sixteen*, Christopher realized. The last time he'd seen her, she'd been a gangly little kid. A sharp pain pierced his heart. It had been hard to leave home. But he had left. For good.

"That was a great nap," Kendra exclaimed, yawning. "I didn't get any sleep on the train because I was sitting next to this huge woman, and she was snoring like an elephant at a watering hole."

Christopher interrupted her nervous ramble. "Kendra, enough," he said firmly. He didn't have the strength for small talk.

Kendra sat down on the couch and stared at the floor.

"Let's get to the point," Christopher stated. "What are you doing here?"

Kendra shrugged. "You're not happy to see me?" she asked.

"That's not the point, Kendra," Christopher groused. "The point is that I wasn't exactly expecting you." Christopher paused. "Does Mom know you're here?"

"I don't really get the sense that she's worrying about that right now," Kendra retorted.

Christopher decided to take a different approach. "Kendra," he said, sitting down next to her. "I have a new life here."

She was silent.

"And I don't want anything to affect it."

"I don't know how I affect your life," Kendra mumbled. "I mean—"

"Kendra," Christopher said, his voice adopting an enigmatic tone. "You know what I'm talking about."

But Kendra just stared ahead, a blank look in her eyes.

"These people know me separate and apart from my old life," Christopher said. "They don't need to know things they're not meant to know."

Is she listening to a word I'm saying? Christopher wondered. *Does she know how crucial it is that my past be kept my past? Does she know how her being here could ruin everything for me?*

That was why he would have to get her away from Chatham Island. And soon.

Zoey

Let's see, my favorite summer memories. I've always loved everything about summer. The smell of suntan lotion. The way it feels to wake up after a nap on the beach.

Writing in my journal next to the open window in my room and hearing kids go crazy when the ice cream truck passes Camden Street.

Kissing Lucas after we've just gotten out of the ocean. The way his lips are freezing cold during our first kiss and all warm once we get going.

My mom's lobster salad.

When I was in eighth grade, I spent the whole summer reading this teen romance series. Every book was about a different boyfriend and girlfriend and how they spent the summer after graduation before they went away and left each other. Sometimes the books ended with the couple getting married. Most often, though, the couple just pledged eternal devotion and did a lot of walking on the beach and a lot of talking about, "Someday when we're together . . ."

I know that series was a total affront to good literature. I mean, the romance novels I write in my spare time are

Shakespeare in comparison, but, funnily enough, I can't help thinking about them now.

Sometimes when I'm going to bed, I imagine that Lucas and I are the main characters in one of the books, and we're saying these old-fashioned things to each other, like, "I'll forever be yours," and "You'll always be my girl," and "You know, you never forget your first love." The book cover has us looking wistful and poetic as we stand on the beach, my white sundress pressed against my body in the ocean breeze, the cuffs of Lucas's jeans rolled up so that they don't get wet.

Pretty pathetic, huh? I don't want to get too far over my head into pop psychology, but is it possible I'm doing all this fantasizing to try to compensate for the current lack of communication in my relationship with Lucas? Because in reality, just one good talk with him would be worth a million flowery speeches and moonlit beaches right now.

Christopher

I BELIEVE IN LIVING FOR
THE PRESENT, SO I DON'T
REALLY LIKE TO CATALOG MY
FAVORITE MEMORIES.

CALL ME A CYNIC; I DON'T KNOW.

I MEAN, I'D SOONER THINK
ABOUT MEMORIES THAT HAVEN'T
BEEN MADE YET. I'D SOONER
THINK ABOUT WHAT WILL HAPPEN
WHEN AISHA AND I HAVE OUR
OWN COTTAGE ON THE BEACH
SOMEWHERE, WHERE WE GO EACH
SUMMER, TAKING THE KIDS AND
THE DOGS. I'D SOONER THINK
ABOUT ALL THAT.

I GUESS I'VE LET MY
MEMORIES OF SUMMERS PAST FADE

AWAY FOR A PURPOSE. YOU KNOW,
I GUESS THEY'RE NOT REALLY
GOOD MEMORIES.

BEING POOR IN THE SUMMER,
WELL, WHAT'S THERE TO TALK
ABOUT? THE FIRE HYDRANTS
THAT YOU OPEN ON THE STREET
JUST TO GET A MOMENT'S BREAK
FROM THE HEAT? THE CAMP FOR
UNDERPRIVILEGED KIDS YOU GO
TO FOR A WEEK, ONLY TO BE
SENT BACK TO THE HELL OF YOUR
REAL LIFE? THE CHEAP LEMONADE
YOU BOUGHT WITH FOOD STAMPS?

I'M SORRY, BUT I'D SOONER
THINK OF SUMMERS TO COME.

Eight

5:00 A.M.

Lucas guzzles down a glass of orange juice. "Eat your eggs," his mother orders. He thinks it's ironic that his mom is treating him like a little kid, when he's waking up at such an ungodly hour to do his father's dirty work.

6:00 A.M.

Lara wakes up to find Nurse Esmerelda's face smiling down at her. *That is literally the most frightening thing I have ever seen,* Lara thinks, her head throbbing. She desperately wants a Bloody Mary.

6:30 A.M.

Jake starts his run down Leeward Drive. He has to work out every day in order to prep for football training camp. Running is not so easy, as he consumed about five Heaven Burgers during his break yesterday. He swears he's not going to have any today.

6:35 A.M.

Benjamin is sitting on the rocks near Town Beach, his surfboard by his side. He's already taken a few hits today, but he plans on going back into the water after he's finished watching the sunrise. It's so amazing to be able to see the sun over the cliffs. It's so amazing to be able to see at all.

7:00 A.M.

Aisha wakes up after having a miserable dream about Christopher and that girl. It was a wedding—her wedding, to be exact—and Aisha was wearing her grandmother's wedding dress, and Nina and Zoey were there as her bridesmaids, and just as she was about to walk down the aisle that girl came running up and began screaming something. Aisha's alarm clock rang before she could hear what the girl was going to say.

7:30 A.M.

Kate wakes up with a start, having just dreamed that she didn't get into any classes. In a daze she runs out to see if the mail is there—the letters regarding class placement should be arriving today. She's outside, in her nightshirt and boxers, when she realizes what's she's doing and that it's not even eight A.M.

8:00 A.M.

Christopher groans at the thought of doing another double shift at Jimmy's, but it's the only way he can make money. At least the breakfast shift is the lightest of them. Christopher has left Kendra sleeping on the pullout sofa in the living room. He hasn't had the heart to kick her out quite yet. He'll give her a couple of days until he sends her home.

8:30 A.M.

Somehow Zoey's clock radio got turned to Light FM, and she ended up waking up to one of Mariah Carey's really slow ballads, which just lulled her back to sleep.

8:45 A.M.

Lucas is taking his first break of the day, having already put in a good three hours' work. On the dock, with the grizzled old fishermen, Lucas feels ill at ease and out of place. "Ya takin' over yer dad's business, aye?" a particularly paunchy lobsterman asks him. Lucas just grunts.

9:00 A.M.

Claire looks out her window to see her dad and Sarah Mendel leaving for the day. Knowing they'll be gone until lunch, she sneaks into the guest room where Aaron is sleeping and wakes him up with a kiss.

9:30 A.M.

Benjamin manages to stay on his board for over three minutes before a wave takes him down. He's out of breath and totally beat . . . but thrilled.

10:00 A.M.

Lara is listening to a lecture about codependency. She feels as though she's going to barf—both from boredom and from breakfast, which was some mealy porridge and bad coffee. She still wants a Bloody Mary.

10:30 A.M.

Zoey wakes up with a start. She can't believe she's slept another two hours. She better call Nina. The two of them are supposed to go job hunting today.

10:31 A.M.

Nina picks up the phone on the eighth ring. *"What?"* she answers. It's Zoey. "A job?" she moans. "Remind me what that is again."

Nina

My favorite summer memories?
Well, here goes. . . . Being able to
watch TV all day. A Cherry Coke
Slurpee. Waking up at noon.

Putting weird combinations of
stuff in my hair and seeing what
happens after I sit out in the sun.

The fact that it's the only time
of the year Claire's hair gets
slightly frizzy.

The way Benjamin's skin smells
when he uses that aloe after-sun
stuff.

Everyone's going on and on about

how this is the last summer. Well,
it's not my "last summer." I'm
not going to college in September.
I'll still be here.

It's not that I don't think
they should be sentimental. I mean,
believe me, I understand. It's just
that, well, I wish they'd remember
not all of us are onward and
upward. I wish they weren't all so
obviously excited about leaving me.

So it's hard for me to get all
nostalgic, to wax poetic, for
summer. I mean, I could spend
this summer counting the days.
Until Benjamin goes away. Until
Aisha and Zoey leave me.

And it's not as if I'll miss Claire or anything. It's just that with all of them gone, I'll be left alone.

Nine

Zoey and Nina stood in front of Fro Go Yogurt.

"No way, Zoey, I am not working there," Nina said indignantly, stomping her combat boots on the pavement and folding her arms.

"Nina, it can't hurt us to apply," Zoey said appealingly.

"Not happening," Nina quipped, turning on her heels.

Zoey sighed. Perhaps her and Nina's idea that they work together over the summer was not a good one. Here she was trying to be as diplomatic as possible, willing to apply for just about any and every job, and Nina was vetoing just about everything. Could Nina be more insanely picky? Every store, every restaurant, every place of possible employment they passed, Nina nixed.

"Come on, Nina, think of all the chocolate yogurt with rainbow sprinkles you could eat," Zoey chided. "It's not like you don't make me come here ten times a day, anyway. If we worked here, at least you'd get a discount," Zoey continued.

"That's the last thing I need . . . to put on the chub," Nina said flatly.

"Nina, as I said on the beach yesterday, you look totally good," Zoey said, shrugging at Nina's newfound paranoia. Nina wasn't usually one to indulge in talk about fat and diets. In fact, Nina usually made it a practice to eat a lot—seemingly without caring. As far as Zoey could tell, eating the grossest, most caloric thing in the cafeteria was Nina's twisted way of being rebellious.

"Whatever," Nina said, doing her best to pull Zoey away from Fro Go. "I'm beat. Let's go get a coffee."

"Nina, you just had a huge cappuccino," Zoey said, laughing. "And we've only walked down two streets."

"Okay, fine," Nina moaned. "But this is totally tedious."

"Wait until you're actually working until you start complaining about tedious," Zoey replied.

Zoey was intent on getting a summer job today, and she didn't have time to idle around looking for the very best one. She needed to make money for next year at college. Of course, she'd help her parents out at their restaurant a few nights a week. But she needed serious money. She needed a day job. After all, she'd just read this magazine that rated Berkeley as one of the most expensive collegiate towns in America. Zoey could only imagine how busy she would be—working on the school paper, course work, sorority rushing. (She hadn't yet admitted to Nina that she was considering the Greek thing.) She didn't want to stress about money the first instant she arrived.

"Okay, Nina," Zoey said, trying to muster up her enthusiasm. "Let's go down Main Street. Maybe, you know, we'll see something there."

"Okay," Nina said reluctantly. "We could just go to the movies, you know," she added, pointing to the mall where the Cineplex was.

"No way." Zoey pulled Nina by the elbow. "How about this place?" She pointed to a secondhand store, the window brimming with vintage wear.

"No can do," Nina said. "The owner of that place hates me 'cause I returned something after wearing it."

"Oh, Nina," Zoey said, sighing. "If it's not one thing, it's another."

Nina grimaced.

"Hey," Zoey said, pointing to a white halter top with sunflowers on it that the store mannequin was wearing. "What do you think of that?"

"Revealing," Nina said.

"Very California, isn't it?" Zoey said.

"I guess." Nina relented. "Whatever that means."

"I can totally see wearing it orientation week!" Zoey said, imagining how amazing the halter top would look with her white jean cutoffs.

"Y'right, whatever," Nina said, evidently annoyed. "You'll be orienting yourself to fun and sun, and I'll still be here . . . in lame Maine."

"Oh, Nina," Zoey said, pulling herself away from the store window and continuing the walk down Main Street. "You'll be out of here soon enough. And anyway, it's not like there's anything *wrong* with Maine. I mean, Lucas is staying here." As she said his name, Zoey felt wistful. *I hope he's okay,* she thought. She and Lucas had barely seen each other since graduation, and Zoey had to admit, she missed him terribly.

"That's good, I guess," Nina responded. "You know, Lucas actually paid me the time of day at graduation. He must have been desperate."

109

"Shut up, Nina," Zoey reprimanded. "Of course he likes you. You're my best friend, after all."

"I know," Nina retorted. "But usually I feel like he wouldn't exactly mind it if I happened to disappear. Like I'm a pain."

"Well, you are a pain!" Zoey teased, putting her arm around Nina's shoulders. "But he still likes you," she added.

Nina shot Zoey a look. "Well, cool, I guess," she muttered.

"I've always thought you guys should be friends independently," Zoey added. "It would be good for Lucas to have more people to talk to."

"I guess," Nina said, shrugging. The two didn't say anything for a while. Zoey was scanning the windows for Help Wanted signs, and Nina just seemed to be staring aimlessly into space.

"Nina, you could at least pretend to look," Zoey scoffed. This was going to be impossible, she thought. Nina Geiger was never going to take looking for a job seriously.

"Hey, look," Nina cried all of a sudden, pointing to a large building looming in the background. "That is our destiny. That's where we should be working!"

Nina was out of her head. The place she

was pointing to was the newly renovated Weymouth Health and Racquet Club, which had just relocated itself to the bottom floor of one of Weymouth's high-rises.

"There!" Nina cried. "We could get in shape! Have free use of the equipment and all. It'll be amazing!"

"Whoa," Zoey said. "I've never seen you this excited before. How do we even know they're taking applications?"

"Let's just go in," Nina pleaded. "You never know."

Zoey was happy to relent, but the whole thing seemed pretty weird.

A health club? That was so *not* Nina. Or was it?

"Now look to the left," the doctor ordered. Benjamin looked to the left. "Now look to the right," the doctor said. Benjamin looked to the right.

"Read the chart in front of you," the doctor bellowed.

"*A-E-T-P-O-R*, I think, *L*, or is that an *I*?" Benjamin went on. He was squinting pretty hard by the time he got to the bottom row.

The doctor nodded and checked off a couple of things on his clipboard. "Okay, Benjamin, could you sit in the waiting room for a few minutes while we prep the next test?" the doctor asked.

"Sure," Benjamin said. He got up and went into the waiting room. His dad was there, sitting on a big red sofa, reading a news magazine.

"How's it going?" Mr. Passmore asked.

"Okay, I guess," Benjamin said, scouring the pile of magazines on the coffee table in front of him for something to read. They were all out of date, of course. Not that that mattered to Benjamin. He was a little out of date himself. The fact that the *People* magazine in front of him was from two months ago didn't much bother him. He hadn't seen a *People* magazine since he was fourteen.

"They're running more tests?" Mr. Passmore asked, closing his magazine.

"Yeah, something like that," Benjamin mumbled. He was reading a story on hairstyles of the stars. It was funny, but it seemed like the same looks he was sporting in junior high were all back. Or was it that they had never gone away? He couldn't be sure.

"Well, the more tests, the better," Mr. Passmore said, adjusting his legs and leaning back in the seat.

"Easy for you to say," Benjamin retorted. "But anyway, I'm fine. I can see everything perfectly clearly now."

"Benjamin, that's not exactly true, is it?" Mr. Passmore shot his son a look of concern.

"It's true," Benjamin said, feeling defensive all of a sudden.

"Benjamin . . . ," his father said. "Be on the level with me. Things aren't perfect."

"Well, Dad, considering I couldn't see anything but darkness for years, things are pretty peachy right now."

"Okay, Benjamin, relax. I just worry about your health. I want to make sure we're doing everything right. And the more tests you have, the better."

Benjamin couldn't figure out why he was being combative with his dad. It seemed that ever since he'd gotten his sight back, everyone was trying to knock him back down, remind him he wasn't out of the clear yet. Couldn't they just let him be happy?

"Benjamin Passmore, we're ready for your second round of tests," the nurse said. Benjamin got up and followed her into another office. It was dark. The doctor was already there, standing in front of a big white screen that was lit from behind.

"Okay, Benjamin, I want you to identify the objects I place in front of the screen. Take your time. What am I holding up?" the doctor asked.

113

Benjamin looked. The object the doctor was holding up was wide at one point and narrow at another. "A frying pan, of course," Benjamin said.

"Okay," the doctor said, putting another item in front of the screen.

"A pencil," Benjamin said listlessly. This was ridiculous. He wanted to get out of here.

After showing Benjamin a few more objects, the doctor turned on the lights. Benjamin's eyelids fluttered as he adjusted to the change. He looked around the office. The nurse was there, her arms folded as she watched the doctor take down more notes.

Displayed on the tray in front of him were the objects he'd held up for Benjamin to identify. Funny, but there wasn't a frying pan or pencil there.

"Obviously things are still blurry," the doctor said, putting down his clipboard and looking Benjamin in the eyes. "But I'm very optimistic that eventually you'll be able to see perfectly."

Benjamin nodded. But this wasn't what he wanted to hear.

"But perfection requires work," the doctor went on.

"Work?" Benjamin asked. He didn't like the sound of this.

"Work," the doctor said definitively. "I'm going to give you a series of exercises to do, and you have to promise me you're going to do them. No slouching, Benjamin."

Benjamin nodded. *Just get me out of here,* he thought.

The doctor continued. "And you have to promise me you're going to take it easy on yourself."

"What do you mean?" Benjamin asked.

"I mean not too much activity. No strenuous activity that requires acute vision. No long movies. Nothing where you have to put too much stress on your eyes."

Benjamin stared at the floor, shuffling his feet.

"Benjamin," the doctor added, raising his voice. "No one's happier than I am that you can see, but that doesn't mean you haven't got a long haul in front of you."

Benjamin nodded.

"The last thing we want to see is a regression of any kind."

Benjamin sat quietly. Even as the doctor took him through what seemed like an endless list of exercises, he was only half listening.

Finally he got the okay to ditch. "See you soon!" he said as he scurried out.

"How'd it go?" his dad asked when Benjamin entered the waiting room.

"Great," Benjamin said. "Let's get out of here."

Ten

When Kate Levin left the Cabrals' house after lunch, she didn't really have a plan. She'd just walk around with her camera, she thought. Taking pictures of whatever jumped out at her, whatever caught her eye.

Kate wandered over to the rocks that overlooked the beach and took pictures of the seagulls who were eating bits of garbage that had been left after a picnic. Then she climbed toward the water and snapped shots of the lighthouse from an angle she'd never gotten before.

Kate stood by the water. It was so calm and soothing, and she loved the way the light changed so frequently. It got breezy, and Kate decided she'd make a move. She'd wait and see where her camera took her.

Sometimes it depressed Kate to have so much time on her hands, but today she felt as though there were a million ways she could fill it. She wondered what Jake was doing now, how he looked, if he was on a break or in the midst of a burger crisis. She decided to head toward the center of town toward Burger Heaven. As she approached the restaurant she felt her heart skipping. *I'm happy,* she thought. *That's all that matters. I'm going to see Jake, and I'm happy. Right now. In this moment.*

Kate started to skip, then, giggling to herself, she slowed to a more dignified gait. When she arrived at Burger Heaven, she peered through the glass pane windows. Jake had a painstaking look on his face as he watched a burger sizzling on the grill. She rapped on the glass to get his attention. When Jake saw her, he smiled. Kate waved and held up her camera. "Is this okay?" she mouthed. Jake shrugged.

Kate started to take pictures. She aimed straight at Jake. It looked cool because the steam from the grill made the glass all foggy and everything behind the pane—even Jake— looked distorted. Kate took shot after shot: capturing Jake's expression as he put mayonnaise on a bun; the busboy as he walked past the window, his hands full of plates; Jake's boss, Max, who looked like he was staring right at her as she snapped the shot. He looked almost hostile, but as far as Kate could tell, that was just his general manner.

Kate was snapping away when she heard a voice behind her. "Getting anything good?" she heard a guy ask. She turned around. It was Benjamin.

"H-Hey," Kate stammered. Benjamin was standing there staring at her, his brown eyes glistening, a smile on his face. Kate still wasn't used to seeing him without his sunglasses on.

"What's up, Kate?" Benjamin asked.

"Not much," Kate answered. She had to admit that Benjamin still made her a little nervous. After all, when she'd been hunting down the guy who'd saved her when she'd gotten caught in the crossfire between Lucas and Aaron, she'd been led to think Benjamin was the guy. Of course, she'd gone for it and completely kissed him. How humiliating to have discovered it wasn't him at all.

"Are you waiting for Jake to get out of work?" Benjamin asked.

Kate was relieved to hear Benjamin mention Jake's name. It gave her an excuse to bring him up herself and let Benjamin know how well things were going. Maybe that would make her feel less embarrassed.

"I'm trying to get a couple of shots of him in action," Kate said. "But I'm sure we'll hang out when he gets off work. You know, we're pretty tight now."

"Got it," Benjamin said, smiling.

"It's all because of you," Kate added. "If I hadn't been such an idiot and gone for you by mistake—"

Benjamin cut her off. "Don't worry about it another second, Kate. It's really no big deal."

Kate smiled and quickly changed the subject. "What do you think of this shot?" she asked, pointing her camera at the window. She ushered Benjamin to come over so he too could peek through the lens.

"What if you got the light coming from that angle over there?" Benjamin suggested, moving the camera slightly toward the left.

"Wow, you're totally right," Kate said, peering through the lens and preparing to take the shot. "You have amazing perspective," she gushed.

"Well, perhaps the fact that I haven't seen for so long changes the way I see things now," Benjamin said, his face breaking into a broad smile.

"Yeah," Kate said. "Do you mind if I ask you a question?"

"Go for it," Benjamin replied.

"Is your vision fully recovered?" Kate asked.

Benjamin hesitated for a moment, then answered, "Just about!"

"Wow," Kate said. "You must be so happy."

"I am," Benjamin answered. "I really am. You know, I'm just trying to do as much as possible. Do all the things I haven't gotten a chance to do for so long."

Kate stared straight ahead. She didn't say anything for a few moments.

"Kate? Are you listening to me?" Benjamin asked.

"So-Sorry," Kate said abruptly.

"I guess it's kind of boring, all this talk of sight and renewed happiness." Benjamin laughed.

"No, no, no," Kate protested. "Not at all. I was just thinking about it. I was thinking that you should do whatever you can to be as happy as possible. You know, just embrace the moment."

"Um, okay," Benjamin said, looking at Kate quizzically. "Maybe if I'm lucky, I'll find something that makes me as happy as photography makes you," he added.

"Maybe," Kate said wistfully. She was probably just tired, fatigued from all the pictures she'd taken that day, but she felt the energy slowly draining out of her. "You know," Kate said thoughtfully, "sometimes it's not so easy to be happy."

"Whoa, I really brought this conversation

down, didn't I?" Benjamin said, laughing awkwardly.

Kate just stared at him. She hadn't realized that she'd said anything strange. But that happened sometimes. She surprised people when she least expected to.

Benjamin cleared his throat. "But you're right—sometimes it's not so easy to be happy."

She peered once more through the window. Jake was watching her again, and when she caught his eye, she felt her face burst into an involuntary smile. *I'm grinning like a fool,* she thought. *A fool in love.*

She threw Jake a kiss and put her camera in its case. *Maybe with Jake in my life, happiness won't be so hard to find anymore.*

Lucas was sick of the smell of dead fish. All day he'd been gathering bait and filling up bags with fish carcasses. He'd hauled so many bags of fish, his arms were killing him, and his lower back was totally aching. For the life of him, Lucas couldn't figure out how his dad had lasted this long before getting injured.

Lucas was standing on the dock, packing up the last of the fish, when he heard Zoey approaching. He could always recognize her footsteps: She walked with a light step, yet it was purposeful, as if she always had somewhere to go. Zoey was holding a large bag from Weymouth Sports Connection in her hands, and she put it down on the dock to give him a kiss and a hug hello.

"Hey, you," she whispered in his ear, giving him a small kiss on his neck.

"Hey," Lucas said, smiling. Zoey always smelled and felt amazing. With her here, he almost forgot about the overpowering stench of fish.

"What'd ya get me?" Lucas teased, motioning toward the bag.

"Well, this leotard would go well with your eyes!" Zoey answered, pulling a royal blue spandex bathing suit–type contraption out of the bag.

"Whoa," Lucas said. "What's that for?"

"Aerobics," Zoey replied. "Nina and I are starting class tomorrow."

Lucas laughed. The idea of Nina Geiger purposely working up a sweat was pretty farfetched. "I thought you guys were going to try to get jobs today," he said. "Instead you got a fitness regimen."

"Well, actually," Zoey said brightly, "we did get jobs . . . at the Weymouth Health and Racquet Club."

"What inspired that?" Lucas asked.

"It was Nina's idea. Don't ask me!" Zoey

shrugged. "But I'm pretty psyched about it. I mean, it will be really good for me to get in shape for California."

California, of course, Lucas thought. These days Zoey couldn't get through a fifteen-minute interval without mentioning the dreaded state.

It was weird, but the minute Zoey mentioned California, the scent of dead fish came back.

"What's wrong?" Zoey asked.

"Nothing," Lucas said.

"I don't believe you," Zoey said. "Are you mad at me?" she asked.

"Zoey, can we not have this conversation again?" Lucas pleaded, looking at her. She looked so downcast, he felt bad. *I can't drag her down to my miserable world,* he thought.

"Lucas, what is it?" Zoey asked. She could never let anything go.

"It just stinks of fish here," Lucas retorted. "I have to get out of here."

"Should I wait for you?" Zoey asked.

Her eyes were filled with concern, and Lucas knew that if he looked into them too deeply, he'd do something crazy, like start to cry or something.

"No, Zo, you should go," he said finally. "I'll see you later."

"I still have party preparations to do," Zoey reminded him. "You could come over?"

"Maybe," Lucas said. "But I'm pretty beat."

"Okay," Zoey said. She picked up her shopping bag. "I'll let you get back to it." She gave him a quick kiss on the cheek and squeezed his hand.

"Later, Zo," Lucas said, watching her as she walked down the dock.

It took him about a half hour to complete all the end-of-the-day chores. He was locking up the boat and gathering up the paperwork he needed to bring back to his dad when Kate showed up.

"Hey, I thought you'd be getting off," Kate said. She was holding up her camera, as if she were about to take a shot.

"Oh, God, don't take any pictures of me." Lucas groaned. "Really, Kate, this is not my shining moment."

"Lucas, come on," Kate said, pointing her camera toward him. Lucas grimaced. "Oh, okay," Kate relented, seeing he really meant what he said.

"What's up?" Lucas asked.

"Nothing," Kate said. "Just got back from home, but I spent most of the day at Burger Heaven."

Lucas nodded. That Jake was probably raking in the dough, he thought, while here he was trudging fish around in the name of family honor. *Another person doing something with his life,* Lucas thought begrudgingly.

"What's going on there?" he asked.

"Not much," Kate answered. "But I got some good news today."

"Oh, yeah?" Lucas wasn't exactly in the mood to hear about other people's prospects, but he knew that Kate didn't have many people to talk to. She was still somewhat of an outsider on Chatham Island.

Kate pulled an envelope out of her pocket. "I got into the most amazing professor's class. It's this guy I've always wanted to work with, Dana Deltori. I mean, he's this total genius." Kate was speaking really quickly all of a sudden.

"That's great, Kate," Lucas said, trying to conjure up as much enthusiasm for his friend and roommate as he could without revealing how secretly annoyed the whole thing made him.

"Thanks, Lucas," Kate said. "Hey, can I help you carry anything?" she asked, watching as Lucas picked up the last of the lobstering equipment.

"No, I can get it," Lucas mumbled.

Kate peered at him, her brow furrowed.

"This is so great that you're doing this for your dad," she said after a moment. "I know he really appreciates it. You're just a really good person to be doing all this," Kate added.

If I'm so good, Lucas thought, *how come I feel so bad?*

Eleven

"We should tell them today," Claire whispered into Aaron's ear.

"I know, I know." Aaron squeezed Claire's pinkie finger.

Claire and Aaron were sitting at a table for four at Il Toro, Weymouth's premiere lunch spot, holding hands under the table. They were waiting for Burke Geiger and Sarah Mendel, who were taking the two of them out for a belated celebration of Claire's graduation. Nina was supposed to come, too, but she'd gotten a job at the health club that started that day. It was probably for the best, though. It would be too strange for Claire to deliver the news about her and Aaron to her dad and Sarah with the forever-jibing Nina present. And Claire didn't want anything to stop her from divulging the truth. The time had come. She was resolute.

"Well, hello, kids," Burke Geiger boomed upon arrival. He was wearing a light blue summer suit and had just come from the bank where he worked. Claire and Aaron untangled their fingers.

"Hi, Dad," she said, standing up to give her dad a kiss on the cheek. "Hey, Sarah," she said breezily, placing an icy kiss on her cheek as well.

"Hello, Claire dear," Sarah said briskly. "And my darling," she said swooping down to give Aaron a hug.

She's going to lose it, Claire thought as she looked Sarah up and down. She was wearing a light lavender knee-length suit with a crisply ironed white blouse underneath. *Like something directly out of the Talbot's catalog,* Claire thought. *She'll never think I'm good enough for her precious son,* Claire figured. The minute they sat down, the waiter arrived. "Hello, Mr. Geiger," he said. "The usual drinks to start?" he asked.

"No, no, no," Mr. Geiger bellowed, his voice awash with pride as he motioned to Claire. "We're here to celebrate my daughter's graduation from high school, and we'd like your finest champagne."

The waiter nodded, jotting down the order on his pad.

"Isn't she a gorgeous girl?" her dad went on, putting the waiter on the spot.

"Dad," Claire whined, casting the waiter a look of sympathy. "How humiliating."

I can't believe that I'm here, about to tell him about me and Aaron, and he's trying to get the waiter to notice my feminine charms. Could things be more twisted?

"Champagne for all!" Burke repeated. The waiter smiled at Claire and walked away.

"Dad, alcohol in the middle of the day?" Claire interrupted. "Sparkling water is fine for me."

"Don't be silly." Mr. Geiger smiled. "You only graduate as valedictorian once."

"Okay," Claire said meekly. She wasn't much of a drinker. She hoped the champagne didn't impair her ability to tell the truth.

The waiter was back in no time. "To Claire." Mr. Geiger raised his glass immediately. "To my beautiful, talented daughter and to her future."

Claire smiled weakly. Her dad seemed so happy with her. She knew he'd feel otherwise once she told him about her and Aaron. *Is he still going to let Aaron live in the house?* she wondered. *I mean, that's the equivalent of letting me live with my boyfriend. He's liberal, but he's not that liberal.*

When they'd all taken their preliminary sips, Claire shot Aaron a look. He shrugged. Claire figured that was his cue to her: She should start.

"Dad, Sarah, I have something to tell you . . . ," Claire stammered.

"What is it, dear?" Sarah asked, absently rapping on her champagne glass with newly manicured pink fingernails.

"We-Well," Claire stuttered. She was about to get the second word of her sentence out when the waiter reappeared.

"Have you had a chance to look at the menus?" he asked.

"Why don't I order for the table?" Burke said, not giving anyone a chance to object. He proceeded to order what seemed to Claire like an endless supply of appetizers and entrées.

Oh, God, we're going to be here forever, she realized. *But there's no going back now. I have to tell them.*

"Burke, you always order too much food," Sarah chastised her new husband.

"It's a celebration," Burke reminded her, putting his arm around her shoulders. "We're going to indulge."

"Your tendency to indulge is not good for your heart," Sarah said, snuggling up to him as she chided him. "All the food you ordered is so high in cholesterol. You know what the doctor said about that—"

"Dad, I—I have something I have to say," Claire interrupted.

"What's that, Claire?" Burke said, smiling. "You want me to cut out the fatty foods, too?"

"No, no," Claire said. "I mean, yeah, sure, if that's what's best for you, but that's not what I wanted to talk about."

"What is it, then, Claire?" Burke asked, smiling benevolently at his daughter.

"I wanted to tell you about me and—" Claire had the sentence almost fully out of her mouth when the waiter abruptly reappeared.

"Courtesy of the chef!" he said, a platter of antipasto in his arms.

"My, my," Burke cried. "They do treat me well here."

"If only you'd treat yourself better," Sarah mumbled, her eyes scanning the platter of oily treats.

The conversation turned to saturated fat again. *Maybe this isn't the time,* Claire thought in desperation. *Maybe I should wait and talk to Dad alone.* She picked up a piece of prosciutto wrapped in a light phyllo dough and put it in her mouth.

"Another toast to Claire!" Burke called out, raising his glass.

Claire sighed. Aaron put his hand on her knee under the table.

*   *   *

"Do you know where the intermediate funk hydro-aerobic class meets?" the petite blond woman in purple spandex asked.

"Down the hall to the left," Nina said, taking the woman's ID card and handing her a towel.

"Thanks!" the woman said cheerily.

"It's my pleasure to serve you," Nina chirped, a huge smile plastered across her face.

"Nina, you should try to at least *sound* sincere," Zoey mumbled under her breath. "Didn't you read the handbook?"

"Yeah, yeah," Nina grumbled. Today was her and Zoey's first day of work at the Weymouth Health and Racquet Club, and Nina was already bored. She'd memorized the schedule of classes, read the handbook over and over again (*Be as enthusiastic as possible. Our clients need as much motivation as they can get!*), and done her turn working at the snack bar. ("Snack" being a generous term for the things they served there—whole wheat bars with mixed berry filling, shakes made from carrot and guava juice, and carob-covered raisins.)

Of all the tasks Nina preferred this one—sitting at the reception desk and taking IDs. At least she didn't have to be on her feet, and she had Zoey there to keep her company. Not that they were chatting that much. Zoey was trying to obey all the rules in the handbook as vigilantly as possible, and rule number four was: *Don't fraternize with your coworkers.*

Every time Nina had tried to strike up a conversation, Zoey hurriedly shushed her. "Jeez, Zoey," Nina had said. "It's not like anyone can see us. I mean, what do you think, Big Brother is watching over us at the health club?" Zoey had just scoffed, looking over her shoulder to see if anyone had overheard.

Nina loved the thought that the Weymouth Health and Racquet Club was like a surveillance society, with some unseen Wizard of Oz–type overlord watching everything they did. Of course, in this case the wizard wouldn't be fat and bald and ruddy faced. He'd be as trim as possible, wearing some kind of stretchy, too-bright unitard with the latest cross trainers on his feet and a perpetual healthy smile lighting up his face.

Nina was imagining herself as one of the evil flying monkeys from Oz. She'd be wearing all black, of course, her hair dyed as dark as possible, and she'd swoop down on the Health and Racquet Club, Twinkies in hand, laughing maniacally all the way.

"Good work, girls." Nina's supervisor broke into her reveries. "I hope you liked your first day," she said.

"Oh, are we off?" Zoey asked, looking at her watch.

The supervisor beamed. "I know," she said. "Doesn't the end of your shift come faster than you think?"

"Uh-huh," Zoey said.

Thank God, Zoey's here to do the kissing butt for us. Because I sure don't have it in me, Nina thought as she began to pack up her backpack. She was thrilled to be getting out of there. *Maybe Zoey and I can stop off at Fro Go Yogurt before the ferry.*

"Nina," Zoey chirped. "I didn't realize we'd get off this early. Now we can make that step class if we hurry!"

"Step class?" Nina said, aghast. "What the—"

"Nina," Zoey reprimanded. "We're here because you so desperately want to get in shape. Remember?"

"Oh, that," Nina said sarcastically. "Well, I don't have clothes with me, so I can't do it."

"You can wear what you're wearing, and I've got an extra pair of sneakers I can lend you," Zoey answered summarily, leading Nina toward the women's locker room.

Nina and Zoey changed as quickly as possible. Of course, Zoey looked amazing in one of the new outfits she'd bought—a light pink spandex top with black bike shorts. It was a far cry from what Nina was wearing—a black T-shirt from an old Elvis Costello concert and Benjamin's old gray sweatpants, which she'd cut off into shorts.

Step class was full of girls just like the ones they'd seen surfing on the beach. They were all really fit and really taut, without a jiggle in sight. *Don't these people have things other than their bodies to attend to?* Nina wondered.

"Let's go stand near the front of the room," Zoey said, pointing to two little purple plastic platforms for them to stand on.

"What are those?" Nina asked.

"Those are the steps, Nina," Zoey said, giggling.

"Oh, like I'm supposed to know," Nina snapped.

"Come on, let's get those places before someone else does," Zoey said.

"Just as long as I'm as far away from the stereo as possible." Nina moaned, covering her ears. If there was one thing she completely and fully hated, it was dance music, and, of course, the aerobics instructor had it blaring. And it wasn't even good dance music, like seventies disco or anything. It was *techno,* the kind of music all those freaky Europeans who didn't know any better listened to. "What do they think this is? A raver?" Nina muttered under her breath.

Nina was brimming with hostility by the time class started. "And one, and two, and kick, and back for more, and one, and two, and kick," the instructor called out in a perky, yet insistent voice. *If she didn't have this hideous music on so loudly, she wouldn't have to scream over it,* Nina thought.

Nina felt her tendons ache after about a minute. She couldn't get the moves right, and she kept tripping over the step. Zoey, on the other hand, acted as though she'd been stepping all her life. Nina couldn't believe how agile she was.

"And three, and four, and kick some more!" the instructor hollered, a wide smile on her face, the dance music blaring.

If this isn't hell, I don't know what is, Nina thought sourly.

"You're doing great!" Zoey nodded encouragement at Nina.

"Just doing what it takes to keep my man," Nina answered wryly.

Zoey grunted. She began to flap her arms up and down, mimicking the instructor. "Why don't you admit that getting in shape is your own personal latest obsession?" she managed between arm waves. "Because Benjamin couldn't care less."

"Zoey, would you stop implying that this is anything less than a full-fledged attempt on my part at changing in order to please my man?" Nina insisted. "I really resent that."

Zoey laughed, not turning her head from the front of the class and the instructor. "Have it your way," she said. "But you're just not sounding like the Nina I know and love."

The instructor and the whole class suddenly turned to the right and began climbing on and off their steps from the side. Nina turned quickly, trying to catch up, and caught the woman next to her in the rib with her elbow. She smiled a sheepish apology. "You're right, Zoey," she said. "This is definitely not me."

She edged her way to the back of the room, and when she got to the door, she called out to the instructor and the class in general, "Have a nice, healthy day, everyone. Just carry on as if I'd never been here in the first place."

She closed the door behind her with a solid thump.

Twelve

Kate was perusing aisle 7 of Weymouth's twenty-four-hour convenience store. This place was one of Kate's preferred destinations in Weymouth—not only did it carry everything from makeup to white T-shirts to magazines, but it also had an amazing section with photo supplies. Kate needed to buy a bunch of stuff for school, which started this evening. Did she have everything she needed? She glanced at her list one more time.

-35 millimeter color film
-Black-and-white transparencies
-Toner for photo development
-Filters for cleaning lens
-Contact sheets

That should be it for school supplies, Kate thought. *I'll pay for this stuff now and then browse the other sections,* she decided.

Kate was standing on line, waiting to pay, thinking about her new class, when she noticed that her professor, Dana Deltori, was standing right in front of her. *Oh, my God,* Kate thought. *Should I say anything?* She wavered momentarily and almost let her shyness get the better of her before deciding to be brave. "Hi, Professor Deltori," she began hesitantly.

"Hello," the professor said, turning around to face Kate. He was a good-looking man with sandy brown hair, probably in his midthirties, wearing a button-down denim shirt with khakis and white tennis sneakers. He had a whimsical expression on his clean-shaven, highly angular face as he waited for Kate to introduce herself.

"S-Sorry," Kate stammered, laughing at herself. "I'm Kate Levin. I'm one of your new students."

"Oh, Kate, yes, hello," the professor said, smiling warmly. "I think I had a look at your portfolio."

"I hope you liked it," she said.

"Well, I admitted you to the class, now, didn't I?" the professor answered.

"Yes, yes, I guess you did," Kate said. *What a stupid thing to have said,* she chastised herself. *But he's not exactly a charmer himself.* "Thank you," she added, lest the professor think she wasn't gracious.

"As I recall, the lines in your photos were very crisp, and you had an interesting use of shadows," the professor said.

"Th-Thanks," Kate stammered. She couldn't believe it. Dana Deltori was a world-class genius. And he was complimenting *her* work.

"Where have you studied?" Professor Deltori asked.

Kate found herself rambling on about her background: about being from New York City, about attending boarding school, about moving to Chatham Island, about art school. By the time she'd told him what course work she'd completed during her freshman year, it was his turn in line to pay.

"Kate, it was lovely meeting you," he said, handing his credit card to the cashier. Kate noticed that he was buying the same development toner as she was, and somehow that made her feel proud.

"Thanks, Professor Deltori. And I'm sorry to have taken up your time," Kate answered apprehensively. She was still thinking about his use of the word *interesting*. That definitely meant something good—she hoped.

"No harm done whatsoever. My pleasure," the professor added. He scooped up his shopping bag. "I'll see you in class this evening," he called on his way out.

Kate paid for her items and moved on to the other side of the store. *That was totally amazing*, she thought. *I mean, I must be the luckiest student in the class—to have had a personal encounter with Deltori before classes started.* Kate walked around the store in somewhat of a daze, looking at all the things she could buy. She couldn't really narrow in on anything, though: She was too dizzy from the experience with Deltori.

Kate found herself in the pharmacy section of the store, staring wistfully at the rows of pills and medications that lined the shelves. She tried to think of them as objects to be photographed. Would she use color film? Black and white? Would she use a telephoto lens? Would she put a bit of gauze over the lens to blur the look of the shot?

Kate stood in place, holding her shopping bags and envisioning potential shots. An old lady almost bumped into her. "Excuse me," the lady said snippily.

Kate stared at her.

"Are you okay?" the woman asked, her tone almost accusatory.

"I'm f-f-fine," Kate said. "Sorry."

The old lady walked away, having jolted Kate out of her daze. *Get a hold of yourself. Don't go there,* she admonished silently.

After all, she thought—looking at the rows of bottles not solely as the object of a potential art shot but as what they were, rows of pills to help ward off sickness and disease—*at least I'm not on medication anymore.*

Lara was sitting in an armchair in the first-floor lounge of the Serenity Hills Rehabilitation Center, bored out of her skull.

I gotta do something, she thought. *Anything to get out of here. Anything to get a drink.*

She looked up to see Umberto walking toward her. Lara knew Umberto was her counselor and that probably he was a pretty straight-edge kind of guy, but she was convinced she'd seen him give her the once-over a couple of times. *He's gotta think I'm cute,* she thought. *I mean, look at the slim pickings going on here,* she mused. *I'm the babe o' the ball.*

"Hey, Umberto," Lara said in her best singsong voice.

"How you doing today, Lara?" Umberto asked.

"Oh, fine," Lara said.

"Really?" Umberto asked, leaning down next to her, his eyes brimming with concern. "That's so wonderful to hear."

"Yeah, I've really been trying to do a lot of thinking," Lara said sweetly. "And, you know, I think I've come to terms with a lot of things."

"Well, Lara, don't push yourself too hard. Take everything slowly, step by step."

"Oh, I am," Lara said, pushing a tousle of hair out of her face and flashing Umberto a look of wide-eyed innocence.

"What are you doing now?" Umberto asked.

Sitting here, thinking about how I'd like to kill each and every one of you. What does it look like I'm doing, idiot? Lara wanted to say.

"Oh, I don't know, just hanging out," she answered. She paused for effect. "I'm feeling a little cooped in, if you must know."

"Cooped in?" Umberto asked.

"You know, it'd be great to see some of the outdoor world," Lara responded, smiling demurely.

"Well, you know you can sit out on the back porch," Umberto pointed out. "Or go out into the yard."

Lara shook her head. "I'd really like to get out out," she said. *Go for it,* she thought. "You know, take a drive or something. . . ." She laid her hand gingerly on Umberto's knee.

Lara watched the color rise in Umberto's cheeks. *Yes,* she thought. *I can see how into me he is. He's totally going to go for it. I can get him to take me to the gas station or something, and I can run into the Quik Mart and get a beer or a wine cooler, anything. Of course, I'll probably have to kiss him or something, but that's okay. It'll be worth it. . . .*

Umberto rose. "Well, Lara," he said haltingly.

"Yes, Umberto?" Lara asked, fluttering her lashes.

Umberto stood there, staring at her. *You know you want me,* Lara willed.

Finally he spoke. "Lara, dear, I'm not about to fall for this. And don't imagine you're the only one to ever try it. These next few days are crucial for you. This is the time to take control. I know it's painful, but this is the most important investment you could ever make—an investment in yourself."

Lara jumped out of her chair. "Don't put the moves on me and then give me that kind of garbage, like you really care," she snapped.

"I'm sorry you feel that way," Umberto responded. "And I'd like to continue our discussion this afternoon during our counseling session. I'll see you later." He turned and walked away without giving even the slightest look back.

"Arrrrrrgh," Lara grumbled to herself. "I cannot believe that."

An immense rage was boiling up inside her. Lara rose and began to pace. She wanted to scream, or tear out her hair, or kill someone, but none of that would get her out of here. Then she saw the phone. There was a big fat guy in the booth, so Lara waited. When it looked as though he wasn't about to move, she slammed her fist on the glass. "Hey, other people are waiting," she screamed. It felt good to let loose a little.

The guy looked at her as if he'd just seen a ghost. "Um, sorry," he said softly. "I'll be off in a second."

"Hurry it up, chubs," Lara muttered under her breath.

When the guy got off the phone, Lara dove into the booth as if it were her last refuge. She picked up the phone and dialed.

"Hi, this is Jenny. How can I help you?" the operator said.

"Yeah, you can help me by doing your job," Lara snapped.

"Excuse me?" the operator asked.

"I want to make a collect call," Lara said. She gave the operator Jake's number.

"Who shall I say is calling?" the operator asked.

Lara paused for a second. "Kate," she answered.

"Thank you, Kate," the operator said. "One moment, please."

Lara could hear Jake's phone ringing. *Pick up the phone*, she muttered under her breath. After the fourth ring he did.

"I have a collect call from Kate," the operator said. "Will you accept the charges?"

"Sure." Lara could hear Jake's voice, confused, on the other end of the line. She waited for the operator to hang up before she spoke.

"Kate?" Jake asked.

"Yes." Lara held her breath.

"Hey, babe," Jake said. "I thought you were on your way to class."

Lara was at a loss for words. The familiarity in Jake's voice, the sweetness . . . it was so vile, it made her completely and totally enraged. He'd never spoken that way to her.

She felt as if she was going to throw up.

Before Jake could say another word, Lara slammed down the phone.

BENJAMIN

Ahhh . . . those golden summer memories!
Lemme tell you, there's nothing like feeling
really hot and sweaty, and being at the beach,
and not being able to go into the ocean
because it's too dangerous for a blind person.

Or hanging out at a pool and having
someone tell you which end is the shallow end.

Or wanting to play tennis but not being
able to see the ball. Or wanting to play
baseball but not being able to see the bat.

Not that I was so into sports when I was
little, before I lost my sight, because I wasn't,
really. I played kickball on the street with my
friends. I went to the pool with my family. I
mostly waded in the ocean; I was always too
scared to go too far out.

And then, by the time I arrived at the stage
where I would have wanted to take a few risks,
maybe get up on a surfboard or something—
poof! It was no longer within my power.

Summer, a time of freedom for most
teenagers, was just a time for me to dwell on
how a part of my freedom had been taken
from me. How it would never be returned.

Only now it has. And I want to make the
most of it. This summer is going to be the
summer I make memories.

Thirteen

Aisha was on the ferry from Weymouth to Chatham Island with what seemed like a million screaming kids. *I'll have to remember to wait for the later ferry next time,* she thought. *That way I'll miss the day camp rush.*

Aisha had enrolled in two college-level physics courses. This way, she figured, she'd already have a head start when she got to college. Her parents were thrilled that she was studying over the summer, and she still would have plenty of free time to hang out with Christopher and her friends. *Not that Christopher would want to spend time with me,* she thought miserably. The last she'd seen of him had been at his building after graduation, when the gorgeous and mysterious stranger had slammed her little body into his. Aisha didn't like to picture this image.

She stayed on board the ferry while the kids deboarded. On land she could see the teeming mass of nannies, parents, and older siblings who were waiting for their charges. *At least I'm not baby-sitting for the summer,* she thought.

She waited for the crowd to thin and made her way off the boat. She'd half expected Christopher would come out to meet her, and she scanned the sea of faces for him. After all, they'd only spoken briefly once since the strange appearance of the mysterious girl. She'd tried to call him at Jimmy's, but he'd been on double shifts and he'd been so busy, he'd barely had a chance to say hello. *Probably I'll see him tonight,* she thought. *Unless I'm deluding myself. Unless he's already run off and married someone else.*

Then she saw him. He was on Dock Street, on one of the benches near the ferry landing.

She walked toward the bench. Yes, it was definitely Christopher. Aisha stopped dead in her tracks.

Because, no, he wasn't alone—he was with the girl from Sunday.

"I've had enough of this," Aisha muttered. "This is out of control." She walked straight up to her fiancé.

"Well, hello there," she said briskly.

"Eesh." Christopher looked startled. And didn't he only grin that sheepish lopsided grin when he was feeling guilty about something?

Aisha inspected his face. *You could introduce us,* she thought angrily. But Christopher just sat there, as if he was waiting for *her* to begin. *Oh, no, Christopher Shupe,* Aisha thought. *I will not make this easy for you.* She glared down at him in stony silence.

"Could you excuse us for a second?" Christopher said, turning to the girl abruptly. He stood up and took Aisha's hand, leading her back toward the ferry landing. Still he kept silent.

"Christopher, look, this is completely insane," Aisha broke out finally. "Who is that girl?"

"Aisha, if I told you it was no one, would you believe me?" Christopher asked haltingly. His face was downcast, and he didn't meet her eye.

"She sure doesn't look like a no one to me," Aisha retorted, glancing back at the girl, who was sitting on the bench reading a magazine, her long curly hair blowing in the ocean breeze, her shapely legs crossed in front of her.

"Aisha, it's someone from a long time ago," Christopher said. "It's no one you have to worry about."

"Christopher, I haven't seen you in two days. I'm sorry, but that makes me worry. And I can't help thinking it has something to do with this stranger!"

"It has nothing to do with her. I've been working, I . . ." Christopher stumbled from

150

word to word, losing track of where he was going midsentence.

"Christopher, this is the weirdest and most outrageous thing ever!" Aisha's voice was rising from hurt and dismissive to complete rage. She was beside herself.

"Eesh, please, give me a chance!" Christopher said.

"No," she said. "*You* come clean. *You* tell *me* what the hell is going on." She sounded like her mother, but she didn't care. Shaking free of Christopher's hand, she turned to walk away. *This can't be happening. This just can't be happening.* Her heart was hammering in her ears.

"Eesh, I'll tell you soon. I swear I'll tell you. It's just that now is not the right time. This has nothing to do with you or with us. Please believe me, Eesh."

Christopher sounded so sincere, so plaintive, she almost relented. But her outrage was too strong. If he had introduced the girl. If the girl wasn't so sexy. It didn't make sense, and she, Aisha Gray, was not about to be duped. She was not one of those women who would put up with anything from a man just because she was in love. She turned off Dock Street on to Climbing Way.

What does it all mean? Aisha wondered as she began to run. She couldn't help thinking her entire engagement was a sham.

*   *   *

It was nine P.M., and Burger Heaven was closed for the night. There were a couple of stragglers finishing up their meals, and Jake was just getting ready to lock the doors. He was about to put the Closed sign in the window when Kate tapped on the glass. Jake unlocked the bolt and opened the door for her.

"Hi," she said, striding in and sitting down at the counter.

"Hey, yourself," Jake answered. As always, he found himself smiling when he looked into her eyes. He had been on cash register duty for the majority of the evening, and he was relieved to have a respite. Especially in the form of Kate. "Not that it's a big deal, but why'd you call me collect earlier and then hang up?" he asked her.

"Huh?" Kate looked up at him blankly. "I didn't do that."

"You didn't?" Jake was confused. *Maybe she just spaced out or something,* he thought. He would have pursued the issue further, but his last customer came up with his check to pay.

Jake rang up the bill. "How was class?" he asked, coming back to the counter.

"Great," Kate said. "The professor's really cool. I ran into him in the drugstore earlier, so I actually got a chance to talk to him one-on-one."

"Great," Jake said. "What's your next project?"

"Landscapes," Kate answered.

Jake never ceased to be amazed by Kate. He loved how seriously she took her work and how confident she was. It made him feel as though he were going out with an adult.

"Don't worry," Kate said. "I'll still come and take your picture while you work."

Jake laughed. "No ego here, Kate. Hey, you wanna split a shake?" he asked.

"Vanilla?" Kate quipped.

"How about a black and white?" Jake suggested. He'd just mastered the art of shake making today, and he was eager to try out what he'd learned.

"Hey, are you sure it's okay with your boss? I mean, I don't want you to get in trouble for slacking off."

"I haven't taken a break yet today," Jake responded bitterly, scooping up some vanilla ice cream and putting it in the blender.

"Oh, okay, I just don't want to get on Max's bad side," Kate said. Jake squeezed what looked like an inordinate amount of chocolate syrup into the mix. "Think that's enough?" he asked.

"Um, yeah." Kate giggled. "I think so."

"I should close this place up for real," Jake said after the last of the customers had left and he had guzzled up the remainder of the syrup from the bottom of the glass.

Kate grabbed her bag. "I can take a hint," she said. She leaned over the counter to give him a kiss good-bye. When Jake returned the kiss, he felt Kate running her fingers gently through his hair, and he could feel the shivers beginning to tingle down his spine. His whole body was melting, as it always did at Kate's slightest touch.

Suddenly Jake heard the back door scrape open, and he jumped down off the counter.

"That's probably Max," he said. "You should get going so I can finish up."

Kate nodded. "I'll come by tomorrow morning," she called, walking toward the front door.

Jake watched the door swing shut behind her. Then he began to go through the day's receipts, tallying up the totals. "Hey, Max," he said when Max emerged from the back room.

Max's face was stern, and he didn't even bother to greet Jake. Instead he said gruffly, "No one's allowed in here after closing time, Jake. No one."

"Sorry, Max," Jake muttered. "I was just on my break."

"Listen, Jake. Your break is a time for you to regain some freshness. To prepare for your next shift. I've always found that meditating during my break helps me gain perspective on the tasks at hand. Ya know what I mean?"

Jake nodded. He tried to look at his watch under the counter without being too obvious.

"Women don't contribute to peace of mind, Jake," Max continued. "They deplete it. Always remember that. Hey, you're a good kid. Get outta here. I'll see you tomorrow."

As Max practically chased him out the door, Jake smothered a smile. Max had obviously not been as lucky as Jake in the romance department. Yes, Kate was a stroke of pure luck. Beautiful, talented, sweet. But Jake would have to remember to tell her not to come by Burger Heaven so often. She obviously had a bad effect on Max.

Fourteen

"And then you would not believe how stupid the women are," Nina was saying. "I mean, this one woman actually asked me if I knew how many calories you burn off when you're in the steam room. I'm like, how the hell do I know? Can you believe that?"

Benjamin didn't say anything.

"I said, Benjamin, can you believe that?" Nina repeated herself.

"Huh?" Benjamin said, turning to her. His attention had been focused on the television set.

"Uch, way to not pay attention to a word I say." Nina flopped a pillow from the Passmores' rec-room sofa into Benjamin's face.

"Sorry," he muttered sheepishly.

Nina knew she should try to be nice. It had been a major effort on her part to get Benjamin to spend the evening hanging out. These days he wasn't satisfied unless he was engaged in some life-affirming activity with a capital *A*. In fact, until about an hour ago he'd had his heart set on going to a laser show at the planetarium in Weymouth. "Oh, please, Benjamin, can't we just hang out normally," Nina had whined. "I mean, it's been about a bazillion years since we've just, you know, sat around, been together."

Benjamin had relented, and Nina had gotten her way. She knew that meant she should be satisfied with the current state of couch potato bliss, but, well, she wasn't. She'd had a rotten day at work, and she had more than a litany of complaints. She wanted indulgence. She also wanted a massage: To say her muscles ached from the step class she and Zoey had taken yesterday would be the understatement of the millennium.

Benjamin was switching channels at a rapid-fire pace. "God, you're like someone who's never seen cable before," Nina'd almost said. She'd stopped herself, thank God. After all, there were a lot more channels now than when Benjamin was last able to see.

"Cool," Benjamin said when he switched to MTV. There was a Garbage video on.

"Since when do you like Garbage?" Nina asked. She glanced at the TV screen critically. "Gross, she's way too skinny," Nina added, pointing to the lead singer.

"You think?" Benjamin said nonchalantly. "I think she kind of looks cool."

"She looks like she's been eating too many mixed berry bars and taking too many hydro-aerobic classes," Nina muttered angrily, resting her feet on the coffee table in front of her.

Benjamin switched the channel again.

"Awesome," he said pointing to the screen. It was a gymnastics exhibition featuring the 1996 U.S. Olympic gymnastics team.

"Benjamin, since when do you like girls' gymnastics?" Nina asked.

"Um, since I can *see* it," Benjamin answered. "Look at how they move around and stuff—it's amazing."

"Uch, they're like these undernourished squeaky-voiced urchins," Nina threw back.

"They're amazing athletes," Benjamin said, leaning forward to get a better look at a bar routine.

Nina sighed. This was putting her in a bad mood. Her quiet night just "spending time" with Benjamin was making her feel competitive and insecure. She knew she was being stupid and selfish, but it was hard not to think that perhaps life had been easier for her when Benjamin couldn't *see* all the girls who were prettier than she was, skinnier than she was, more talented than she was.

Get a grip, she told herself. *Stop acting like you believe every* Cosmo *article you read.*

Benjamin turned the channel again. "Oh, my God, Nina, is this *Baywatch*?" he asked. She looked at the screen: Pamela Anderson Lee was frolicking on the beach in her trademark red one-piece, her breasts almost fully exposed.

Nina groaned.

"Cool!" Benjamin said. "After all these years of just hearing the voices, I can finally see what these people actually look like. This is hysterical!"

"Just smashing," Nina grumbled, watching intently as Pamela ran into the water in an attempt to save a drowning child. Her bathing suit was so tiny, you could practically see her entire butt.

Nina groaned. *I'm definitely going to go to a stretch class tomorrow. Even if it kills me.*

"Lucas, I'm so glad you're here," Zoey said. Lucas had come over after work, and he was lying facedown on Zoey's bed.

Zoey was in the middle of making a mixed tape for her party, going through her CDs, picking out songs and listening to them as she dubbed them. She loved the whole process, but she'd turned off the music when Lucas arrived.

Now Lucas kept his face hidden in the pillows at the head of her bed. "I am so dead tired," he said, so low it was almost a whisper.

Zoey dropped the CD out of her hand and went to Lucas. She stroked his hair and began rubbing his shoulders. "Lucas, you know, you can talk to me about whatever it is you're feeling. I mean, we've barely talked about what working for your dad is actually like. . . ."

"What's to talk about?" Lucas asked. "Work is work."

"I know you hate it," Zoey said. "But maybe there's some way for you to get out of it."

"No such luck." Lucas sighed, resting his head on Zoey's shoulder. "I mean, I guess my dad could have some miraculous recovery or something, but that doesn't look likely."

Zoey kissed the top of Lucas's head. His hair smelled like sea salt. "How is your dad?" she asked.

"He barely leaves his bedroom. But that's probably because he's discovered how much he likes ordering my mom around all day long, asking her for tea and complaining that the house is too cold. It's been too damn cold for my entire life, but this is practically the only time my dad's ever spent in it, except a few hours at night in a dead sleep."

Zoey touched his chin with her index

finger. "I know how hard this is for you. But it's not forever," she said.

"No," Lucas said. "But it *is* six weeks, and by the time that's over . . . you'll almost be gone. So it might as well be forever." He had raised his head and turned to talk to her, but now he sank back down into the sheets.

Zoey felt as if her heart would break. "I know," she said. "I've thought of that."

"I hate thinking of my life without you," Lucas said.

Zoey felt a determination rise within her. "Lucas, I want to make a pact," she began.

"What are you talking about?"

Zoey's mind was racing. "I want to make sure we spend as much time together as possible. I don't want to lose any time. I want this to be *our* summer, Lucas."

"I want that, too," Lucas whispered. "I just hope I can be in a good enough mood for you."

"Lucas, just as long as you're with me, I don't care what mood you're in."

Zoey felt pierced by guilt. Here she'd been so excited about going away, she'd forgotten that she'd be leaving Lucas behind. She'd forgotten how much it would hurt. And Lucas had been hurting all along.

Fifteen

Kate was deeply immersed in the second chapter of the *History of Photography* when the phone rang. She thought about not answering it. After all, her first assignment—a two-page essay on the use of landscape in depression-era photography—for Mr. Deltori's class was due tomorrow. She was going to have to shoot her own series about modern-day landscapes soon, and not only did she have to write this general essay tonight but she also had to formulate some idea about what her own series of photographs would be.

It might be Jake, Kate thought as the phone rang a third time. She put down her book and went to answer it.

"Hello, Kate." It wasn't Jake. It was her mom.

Kate groaned. If there was ever a reason not to answer the phone, this was it.

"Hi, Mom," she said, putting on her best cheery voice.

"Kate, dear, are you working?"

"Yes, Mom," Kate answered. "In fact, I kinda have to get back to it." She was trying to keep the conversation short.

"Oh, well, it won't hurt you to talk to your mother for a few minutes, will it?" her mother said. Kate could feel the guilt transmitting itself through the telephone wires.

"No, of course not, Mom," she answered sweetly. "I just don't want to stay up too late, you know."

"Did you get into the course you wanted?" her mom asked.

"Yeah. It's really great, actually. The professor's amazing. He's really smart and really cool."

"Cool?" Kate's mom said critically. "I hope you don't use the word *cool* in front of your professor."

"No, Mom, actually I don't," Kate said. "I really should get back to work," she repeated.

"Well, you shouldn't have left your assignment until the last minute. If you don't mind my saying so," her mother reprimanded.

I do mind your saying so, Kate thought.

Kate took a deep breath. "Well," she began. "I didn't. We only got the assignment yesterday, and I had other work to do, and—"

"You know what your father always says: Discipline is the root of all success. Oh, here he is. He just walked in the door." Kate could hear her mother greeting her dad in the background. "I'd better get going," she said. "Good luck with your assignment."

Thank God, that's over, Kate muttered to herself as she hung up the phone.

She went back to her desk and to the book that was lying there. She looked at the clock. *If I start writing in a half hour and it takes me two hours to complete the essay and two hours to formulate my own project, then I'll still get to bed by one in the morning,* she thought.

Kate stared at the page she'd just been immersed in moments ago, but somehow the words seemed to just stare back her. They were like a big, tangled, jumbled mess, incomprehensible. *Forget going to bed by one.* Kate gasped. *I'm going to be up all night, if I get this done at all.*

How come she was suddenly feeling so horrible? *I never should have answered the phone,* she reprimanded herself. *It's my own fault, too. I wanted to talk to Jake, I wanted to procrastinate. I got what I deserve.*

Kate held her head in her hands and tried to get ahold of herself. What was it her therapist used to say about not letting her mother get to her? What was it her therapist used to say about the pressure she put on herself?

Somehow—over the course of the last few months—she'd let herself forget that she'd been on antidepressants. There was no reason to have thought about it on Chatham Island—until now.

I really shouldn't have answered the phone.

"Christopher Shupe, you have one minute to explain. Otherwise I'm leaving," Aisha said, staring at her fiancé over the table, her arms folded across her chest.

Neither Christopher nor Aisha had touched any of the food on their plates.

"Eesh, wouldn't it be possible to talk about something else?" Christopher pleaded. "You haven't even told me anything about your courses. How are they going?"

"Don't even try to change the subject," Aisha snapped. "Christopher, I'm serious. I want answers, and I want them now. I only agreed to meet you so that we could get things straight."

"Eesh, I . . ." But Christopher didn't finish his sentence. He looked down at his plate. "I can't . . ."

Aisha knew she wasn't making this easy for him, but why should she? If their marriage was going to work, their engagement was going to have to work first, and as far as she was concerned, this was not working.

"Eesh," Christopher began again, "you're just going to have to trust me."

"No can do, Christopher," Aisha said. She knew she shouldn't have said that. Christopher had trusted *her*. He had taken her back after the David Barnes debacle. Well, perhaps she just wasn't as generous a spirit.

"Aisha, come on, just let it rest," Christopher begged. "There are things about me, I—"

"Things about you what?" Aisha asked. "What is it, Christopher? Is that your girl-friend from the army or something? Are you sleeping with her?" Aisha was beginning to feel hysterical.

"No, Eesh, it's nothing like that," Christopher said emphatically. "For the last time, I told you, she's not someone you have to worry about."

Aisha couldn't believe how sick she was of hearing him tell her not to be worried. Clearly it was too late for that. She was already worried. "I'm out of here," she muttered.

"Eesh, please!" Christopher moaned.

Aisha stood up. "Here we go again," she said, picking up her bag and stomping out of the restaurant. This was the second time in two days she'd left him midsentence.

Aisha started her walk down Climbing Way. It was dark already, and the night had turned chilly. Aisha had walked this way a thousand times before, but she still felt creeped out on the deserted road.

She walked briskly and purposefully. *I want to be home to think about all this,* she thought. *Not to mention the fact that I'm completely starving.* Up ahead she noticed a shadowy figure coming toward her on the other side of the street. Aisha recognized everyone who used Climbing Way, and this was a stranger.

She squinted to get a closer look and felt her heart skip a beat. It was the girl, Christopher's mystery girl, and she was walking straight toward Aisha.

Oh, my God, Aisha thought. *Here's my chance.*

"Hey," she called out. But the girl kept walking. Aisha called her again. "Wait, please!"

The girl turned and faced Aisha. Aisha could see the flash of recognition in the girl's huge brown eyes. Then the stranger speeded up. *She's trying to avoid me,* Aisha realized. *You're not getting away that fast.* She dashed toward the girl and waved her arms.

But just as Aisha was about to cross Climbing Way, a car came barreling toward her. Aisha ducked back to her side of the street. By the time the car had passed, the girl was gone.

For a second Aisha wondered if she'd actually seen her.

Sixteen

For the first time since she'd arrived at the Serenity Hills Rehabilitation Center, Lara woke up *without* a pounding headache. Her forehead felt tight and sore, but she didn't have the heinous migraine she was accustomed to waking up with these days.

And for the first time since she'd arrived at the Serenity Hills Rehabilitation Center, Lara woke up *without* desperately wanting a drink. It wasn't that images of Bloody Marys and screwdrivers and gin and tonics weren't coursing through her mind. It was just that they weren't the first visuals to flood her waking brain.

First were the images from her previous night's dreams. She'd had an entire series of them, all about Chatham Island, all featuring the same set of characters, among them: her parents, Zoey, Benjamin, and Jake.

Lara grabbed for the notebook the counselors insisted she keep by her bed. They'd told her that if she remembered her dreams, she should record them.

Lara opened the notebook and stared at the pages. She picked up a pen.

DREAM #1
There was a birthday party, and it was my birthday party, and I was wearing this really amazing all-black skintight outfit with really high heels, and it was totally awesome, and I was having the best time.

There was a huge cake that Mrs. Passmore carried out. It was white and pink with yellow roses, and it said, We Love You, Lara, on it. I was so happy. Then Mr. Passmore came out with a gift for me. It was a small, royal blue velvet covered little box, and inside it there was a pair of little diamond earrings.

I put them on and said, "Thank you, Daddy," and he said, "Anything for you, princess." And then Benjamin came over to me and told me I was his favorite sister, and I giggled and gave him a big kiss on the cheek.

Jake was sitting next to me the whole time, holding my hand. I said, "I love you, Jake," and he looked me in the eye and said, "I've al-ways loved you, Zoey." And I said, "Funny joke," and he looked at me all weird.

Then everything started to feel really eery. I looked at the cake, and it didn't say what I thought it said. It said, We Love You, Zoey. And all the place mats said Zoey on them. And then Mr. Passmore started singing, "Happy Birthday," but when he got to the name part, he said Zoey's and not mine.

Then I woke up.

DREAM #2

I had a dream that I was running down this mountain path, and it was raining out. I realized that I was chasing someone, but I couldn't figure out who it was. When I got closer, I recognized the person I was chasing was Zoey.

I screamed, "It's all your fault, all of it."

I pushed her, but I woke up before I could see whether she had fallen.

DREAM #3

I was making this sculpture with red clay, and I was having a glass of champagne, and it was funny, but every time I took a sip of champagne, a bit of the sculpture would fall off.

And suddenly I realized that the sculpture I was making was of myself, and each time I

*took a sip of the drink, a different part of my
body or a feature on my face would fall off.*

It was really creepy.

I woke up thinking I should stop drinking.

Lara slammed the book shut. *I've been so
abused . . . by everyone*, she thought. *By Jake.
By my parents. By my so-called sister, Zoey.
I've been terribly mistreated.*

Lara pulled herself out of bed and threw a
robe on over the Serenity Hills t-shirt she'd
worn to bed. She ran out of the room and
down the hallway to the lounge. She was
barefoot.

When she got to the phone booth, she saw
that the same guy who'd been using it before
was there again.

"Listen, whiner, I need this phone now!"
she said as authoritatively as she could.

"Jeez, I was just getting off," the guy said
as he emerged from the booth. "You don't
have to be so hostile."

"Oh, yes, I do," Lara mumbled.

She ensconced herself in the booth, only
to find that the guy had left his calling card
there. "At least he was good for something,"
she said bitterly, plugging in the numbers.

She called her dad's restaurant but got the
recording. Then she called her house. She

hoped her dad would answer because she'd tell him to come and get her right now. She was sober, and she was pissed. She wanted out. The phone rang about five times. Finally someone picked up. It was Zoey.

"Hello?" Zoey said. Lara felt ill just hearing the saccharine tone of voice.

"Uch," she muttered and hung up.

Might as well try Jake again, she thought.

Lara dialed Jake's number. "Is Jake there?" she asked when his dad answered.

"Nope," Mr. McRoyan said. "He's at work, at that burger place."

Burger place, burger place, Lara thought, trying to drum up the name of any of the joints she'd heard of on Chatham Island. *Oh, I know—Burger Heaven.*

Lara called information and got the number. She dialed it immediately and waited for someone to pick up. "Burger Heaven," a gruff voice answered.

"Can I talk to Jake?" she asked.

"Who?"

"Jake," Lara screamed. *You stupid idiot, if I scream any louder, the entire hall is going to wake up.*

"Don't get all uppity, missy," the guy yelled back. "I'll get Jake, but he knows he's not supposed to be getting personal calls at work."

173

Like I care, Lara thought. There was a ton of noise—plates banging, trays being piled on top of one another, doors slamming—but she heard Jake's boss calling for him.

"Hey, Jake, your girlfriend's on the phone again."

Your girlfriend? Lara thought. *He thinks I'm Kate.*

Without thinking, she slammed the phone back down. Her hands were shaking.

Everything was so out of control. And she wouldn't be able to do anything about it until she got back to Chatham Island.

"Kid, did you hear what I said? You got a call!" Max screamed across the restaurant.

"Damn," Jake muttered. He was in the middle of making a burger medium rare, and if he ran to take a call, it'd be medium well by the time he came back.

"Kid, it's your girlfriend calling . . . again," Max hollered. Customers were looking at him now. What could he do? He couldn't ask Max to take a message.

So Jake forsook the burger and ran to the pay phone. "Thanks, Max," he muttered, and picked up the line.

It was dead.

"What the hell?" Jake said, hanging up the

phone. By the time he got back to the grill, his burger was on its way from medium well to charbroiled. And Max was standing there, watching it.

"Kid, look, I like you, but you and your girlfriend have got to cool it," Max said.

"But Max . . ." Jake struggled for words. "That wasn't my girlfriend on the phone."

"Y'right, kid. Look, no one appreciates young love more than I do, but I can't have burgers burning on account of it, if you know what I mean."

Jake nodded.

"I've told you I don't want her hanging around here anymore. And no more phone calls, either. Okay? Like I said, it distracts you, and it distracts the customers."

"B-B-But," Jake sputtered.

"No buts," Max said firmly. "I told you I don't go for flakes, and love-lost teens are usually the flakiest of all."

"Okay," Jake said. *It's easier to agree.*

"I'm glad we had this talk, kid," Max said. He walked away.

"But it wasn't my girlfriend," Jake mumbled under his breath.

Seventeen

"Wait, what's the T-zone again?" Aisha whispered to Zoey.

"I think it's the part of skin over your eyes and then down your nose," Zoey whispered back. She thought about it for a second. "But I'm not sure," she added.

"This is all beyond me," Aisha said, shrugging. "I shouldn't have come."

"Oh, come on, Eesh, it can't hurt. And it's free," Zoey said, referring to the makeovers the Weymouth department store was giving. One of the clients at the Health and Racquet Club had told her about it. It was Nina's and her lunch break, and Aisha had met them before her physics course started.

"Look," Zoey continued. "Even Nina's enjoying it."

Nina was sitting in a big white chair, her head tilted back, her eyes closed as the makeup artist sloshed a tinted moisturizer all over her face. "You just need a little coverage over your trouble spots," the makeup artist was saying.

"Read: We just need to throw a little plaster on your face so we can paint over it, and you'll never see your zits again," Nina retorted. The makeup artist laughed.

Well, at least she's amused and not annoyed, Zoey thought, relieved. Bringing Nina to something like this was always an iffy proposition. You never knew how she was going to behave. Zoey was shocked at how open Nina was to all the makeup artist's ideas and treatments, but her increasing consciousness about her looks was probably to blame. *If only Nina could see herself for what she is,* Zoey thought. *She's absolutely and completely adorable.*

As for herself, Zoey needed to fill the time until Lucas would get off work. She'd decided to try for a new look. All her life she'd been doing a preppy, somewhat conservative look (melon-colored blush, a tiny bit of mascara, peach-tinted lip glosses), and now that she was moving out to California, she wanted to be a little more adventuresome. She was hoping to find some pastel nail polish. Or at least some white eyeliner, even though that was very Janet Jackson, circa 1995.

She was even contemplating getting that

sunflower-covered halter top she and Nina had spotted at the secondhand store on Main Street. That would be a great party outfit.

"I wonder if this woman could give me some tips on my hair," Aisha said.

"Of course she could," Zoey responded. "But Eesh, what's wrong with your hair? It's totally gorgeous."

"You should see that girl's hair," Aisha said wistfully. "I mean, talk about phenomenal."

"Oh, Eesh," Zoey said sympathetically. "I'm sure she's not all that you say she is."

"Whatever," Aisha said. "Talk to me about it after you've seen her."

Just then, Nina emerged from the makeup chair. "What do you guys think?" she asked.

"Wow," was all Zoey could think to say. "You look amazing, Nina."

Nina's lips were a dark berry color, and she had on the light blue eye shadow that all the magazines were featuring. You couldn't see a spot or a zit if you had a magnifying glass.

"How much does all that cost?" Aisha asked under her breath.

"Whatever it is, it's worth it," Nina said, staring at herself in the mirror.

"Nina, but do you think you can do that

yourself?" Zoey asked. She hated to burst Nina's bubble, but she sincerely doubted Nina would be able to make the same magic the cosmetician had.

"It's easy. I'm an artist," Nina said.

"Whatever you say." Zoey giggled. She climbed up onto the makeup chair.

"Oooh, look at that gorgeous peaches and cream complexion," the makeup artist marveled.

"I'm having a party on Saturday, and I want to try out a new look," Zoey explained. *Lucas will be so surprised,* she thought.

By the time Zoey emerged from the chair, she had eighty-five dollars' worth of new product on her face. Plus the woman had convinced her to try false eyelashes. "Are you sure this is hip?" she'd asked.

"Oh, yes, definitely," the woman had said.

Zoey and Nina perused the facial cleansers while Aisha took her turn. "I guess my skin's a little dry, yeah," Zoey could hear Aisha telling the woman. "No, I don't use a toner," she went on.

"We're all going to look amazing at this party," Zoey said gleefully to Nina.

"I guess," Nina said. "Maybe I just won't take this off until then."

"Nina, something tells me that's not exactly sanitary." Zoey laughed.

But when Aisha was finally done and the three had rung up their bills, Zoey felt a pang of sadness. No amount of makeup, no new look was going to fix things between her and Lucas. And she hadn't meant to spend that much money, anyway. Especially considering that she was making so little now and that she'd need so much for school in the fall.

"I hate to say this," Aisha said, surveying her bag of purchases as they walked out of the store. "But I already feel regretful."

"Yeah," Zoey added, fiddling with her false eyelashes.

"Is anyone itching?" Nina asked. "I don't know, but my face doesn't feel right."

Nothing really feels quite right anymore, Zoey added silently. *I have to face the fact that I'm going away.*

"Kendra, I told you not to come and bother me at work," Christopher scolded his sister.

"I'm sorry, Christopher, but you were asleep when I got home last night, and I have to talk to you," Kendra insisted, twirling a ringlet of dark hair around her finger.

"Fine." Christopher sighed. "What in the world is it?"

"It's your girlfriend," Kendra said.

Christopher felt his face go rigid, but he

180

tried to appear relaxed. He forced himself to smile. "What about my girlfriend?" Christopher asked.

"I saw her last night," Kendra said quietly.

"*What?*" Christopher said, his voice quivering with anger. It was pointless to continue to play it cool. "Well, I hope you didn't talk to her, like I told you not to."

"I didn't," Kendra said pleadingly. "But it was terrible. I mean, she called to me, and I ran away. She probably thinks I'm the biggest idiot."

Christopher sighed. He didn't know how much longer he could keep this up. Either he had to explain to Aisha that Kendra was his sister visiting from home and get into a long entangled story about his past or Kendra had to leave . . . now.

"Kendra, I think this is an indication that it's time for you to go home," Christopher said. He tried to adopt as kind a tone of voice as possible.

"That's not happening, big brother," Kendra said.

"Excuse me?" Christopher asked. He hadn't expected her to act so obstinately.

"What I said," Kendra insisted. "I'm not going home."

"What do you mean, you're not going

home?" Christopher asked incredulously. "You have to. It's not an option to stay here."

"It is, too," Kendra said firmly. "And I dare you to call Mom about it. I promise you she won't care."

"Kendra!" Christopher bellowed. "You will be going home. I don't care how stubborn you are."

He waited to see if he'd have any effect on her this time, but it wasn't looking good. Sometimes Kendra could be as pigheaded as . . . well, as he could be himself.

"Nope," Kendra said. "And I'm not lying for you anymore. Next time I see your girl-friend—who's very pretty, by the way—I'm introducing myself. I mean, if you're going to marry her, she's going to be my sister-in-law. And that's family, isn't it?"

Christopher knew it was pointless to argue. He could feel everything he'd worked so hard for evaporating before his eyes. He could feel his past rushing up to engulf him. And he could feel his future slipping away.

Eighteen

Benjamin had gotten up with the sun. It was Friday morning, and this was the day all the surfers came out superearly. Benjamin had been at it for almost a week now and felt like it was about time for him to really go for it.

He'd guzzled down an extrastrong cup of coffee, grabbed his board, and walked down to the ocean. When he'd made it down to the shore, he'd gotten a lot of "Hey, dudes" from the other surfers. He loved the idea that he was a regular boarder.

"It's kinda rough today, man," one of the burlier of the guys said to Benjamin.

"And the sun's kicking in kinda early," another one said.

Benjamin was unperturbed. "It's okay," he said. "I'm going for it."

"Cool, dude," the two guys said in unison.

The three of them entered the water at once, Benjamin trailing behind the others as they doggie-paddled, boards in tow, out into the ocean.

"See you on shore, dude!" the surfers cried, taking the first wave. Benjamin waited for the next one.

"Looks like a biggie," a girl said. Benjamin recognized her from last Sunday when he'd come down to the beach with Nina.

"Yeah, no problem," Benjamin said, smiling. The girl smiled back.

The wave hit, and Benjamin was flying. *This is what it's all about,* he thought as he rode the crest of the wave, his arms out, knees bent. *What a high.*

Benjamin's mind was racing. What had those guys been thinking when they warned him about it being a difficult surfing day? It was amazing out.

The doctor had also warned him, had told him to take it easy. But Benjamin wasn't about to forgo an opportunity like this one, an opportunity to fly. All at once he realized he'd lost his footing a tiny bit. He could feel the board slightly pulling out from underneath him and knew he had to try to regain his balance if he wanted to stay afloat.

But regaining his balance required looking at the placement of his footing, and with the fierce glare from the sun, that was an impossibility. Benjamin squinted and blinked, but it was no use: Everything was blurry. He couldn't tell where his feet were in proportion to the board, and he couldn't see in front of him, to see where the wave ended and the shore began.

Benjamin felt himself getting pulled under the current, and he held his breath. Suddenly a wall of harsh icy water slammed over his head. It reminded him of riding the waves as a little kid and getting turned over in the tide. His face scraped against the shore, and his mouth was filled with salt.

Benjamin struggled to resurface, gulping in a huge mouthful of air as soon as he could. Then he stood up, panting, and swirled his head around to get his bearings again.

"Whoa, dude, you okay?" one of the surfers asked as Benjamin trudged up to shore, dragging his board behind him.

"That's a big bruise," the surfer girl he'd seen in the water said, motioning for Benjamin to look at his calf. And indeed, there was a large black-and-blue mark beginning to form.

Benjamin lay down on his towel. It hurt to breathe. Everything was a little blurry.

"Dude, better luck next time," someone

called out. Benjamin tried his best to smile.

Next time, he thought. *I don't know if there's gonna be a next time. I mean, I am not ready to lose my sight all over again.*

Lucas was spent. He was sitting on the dock, dangling his feet off, just staring into space. After an eight-hour shift that started at five A.M., how could he have the energy to do anything else?

So, as happy as he was to see Zoey walking toward him, looking as pretty as ever in one of her new exercise outfits, her face aglow, he still didn't want to do what she wanted him to do, which was accompany her onto the ferry and to Weymouth, where they were going to buy for the party.

"Come on, Lucas. It'll take less than an hour," Zoey was pleading.

"No, it won't, Zo," Lucas said. "I *know* what shopping with you is like. *Nothing* takes an hour."

"Well, actually, I'm limited in terms of time," Zoey admitted. "I have to be at work in two hours, so, you see, there's no way you can get stuck at the store for too long."

Zoey looked up at him with her big eyes, and he couldn't resist. He had to admit he missed spending time with her. And he did feel a little bad that all he'd done when they'd hung out in her room was crash on her bed.

"Okay," Lucas said. "But let's *please* not drag it out."

Zoey kissed him. "Thank you," she said.

Lucas and Zoey rushed to get on the ferry and get into town. In no time they were perusing aisle 9 of the Weymouth convenience store.

"What do you think of pink-and-yellow-striped plates?" Zoey asked.

"Sure," Lucas said.

"Lucas, you're not even looking at them," Zoey insisted.

"Zo, come on, I'm a guy. What do I know? I'm sure they're fine." The truth was that all he could think about were his aching muscles. He hoped his dad wouldn't call him into his bedroom when he got home for a report on that day's haul, as he sometimes did.

"I really think this party's gonna be great," Zoey was saying. "I think it's going to put a good end to the year."

"Right," Lucas said. *Somehow I have to muster some excitement about this thing.* He nodded. *Is this how my dad feels with my mom?* he wondered.

Zoey spent what seemed to Lucas like an inordinate amount of time choosing tablecloths and napkins. He felt as if he were going to collapse on his feet.

"Zo, don't you need to get to work?" Lucas asked, looking up at the clock above the register.

"Oh, my God, I do!" Zoey squealed, throwing some tablecloths into the already overflowing cart. "I can't believe I lost track of the time! Lucas, would it be okay if maybe you walked me to work?" she asked. "I mean, there's no way I can carry this all there myself."

Nina Geiger was sitting behind the reception desk when they reached the club.

"Hey, Nina, we got all this party stuff!" Zoey said.

"Excellent," Nina said. "Except that I won't be there."

"Excuse me?" Zoey replied as she started to put the bags underneath the reception desk.

"Zoey, hello, an alien has taken over my face. Check it out," Nina said, pointing to what looked to Lucas like an inordinately big blotch on her face. "Neither of us will be able to attend."

"Ouch," Lucas said.

"It'll clear up," Zoey said soothingly.

"Yeah, right." Nina snorted. "Anyway, me and Cousin Zit are going to take a break and go get McDonalds."

Lucas smirked. "I'll walk out with you, Nina," he said. Then turned to kiss Zoey good-bye.

She was standing behind the reception desk surrounded by photos of toned and glowing models in skimpy workout gear, pale by comparison and slight. Her cheeks were flushed, and her hair was beginning to take on the yellow summery glow he'd noticed it acquired every summer since his childhood. She looked like a blond angel. And he didn't know how he could have been stupid enough to waste one single minute with her worrying about his father, and lobsters, and next fall.

Nineteen

Kate's stomach hurt as she waited for Mr. Deltori to call her name. Her hands were icy cold.

One by one the students were going up to the professor's desk to get their essays back. Kate wished she'd been first so she could just have it over with.

Kate couldn't say she was exactly pleased with the work she'd turned in, but by the time she'd actually completed the assignment, she was just happy to have something finished.

It had been a long night, and Kate would just as soon put it out of her mind forever. She'd stayed up until four A.M. (And Kate was *not* a late night person.) She'd alternated between crying and writing. Of course, the crying had been easier than the writing. Every time she'd committed something to the page, she'd been convinced it wasn't good enough and thrown it out.

The whole thing had been more than grueling. And for what? An essay that Kate was, well, embarrassed about. Of course she almost always felt that way about her work until she received encouragement from a viewer.

Maybe he took pity on me because it was the first assignment, Kate tried to reassure herself. *Or maybe it's not as bad as I think it is. Maybe I just have no critical faculties. I can't judge myself. . . .*

Kate's head was full of potential scenarios when Mr. Deltori called her to his desk. She grabbed her books and backpack and headed to the front of the room.

"Hi, Mr. Deltori," she said. She kept her head down.

"Kate, I have your essay for you," he said. "I can't say I didn't expect better of you," the professor continued. Kate heard the disappointment in his voice. She looked at her paper.

Written at the top of the page it said: *Grade: C. Kate, please discuss with me.*

Kate felt the color come to her cheeks. She was horrified. She'd thought she'd get a B. Even a B minus would have floored her. But a C!

She slunk out of the classroom and ran to

the ferry. The ferry was crowded, but Kate managed to find a corner in which to hide. *I have to talk to Jake,* she told herself. *I just need to talk this out with someone.*

When she got to Weymouth, she headed straight to Burger Heaven. Thank God, Jake was right there at the counter. He was standing next to his boss, who just looked at her.

"Hey," she said breathlessly.

"Hey, Kate." There was something hesitant in Jake's manner. A certain reserve, almost a coldness.

"Jake, I have to talk to you," Kate cried. "It's . . . everything's going wrong. I got into this thing with my mother, and then I did horribly on this paper for class, and I don't know what to do."

Kate felt like she was losing control. Words were just pouring out of her mouth. She didn't even know if she made any sense, and Jake didn't respond. *Is he mad at me?* She searched her memory, urgently trying to recall the last time she'd talked to him. He had been so sweet then. He hadn't seemed angry at all. What was going on?

"Kate," he said, "can we talk about this later?" He spoke slowly and deliberately.

"Jake, I—I'm really upset," Kate stammered incredulously.

"Kate," Jake said, his voice softening, "there's nothing I can do about it *now*." He gave her a funny look and shook his head. "I'll talk to you later," Jake added, a strange grin crossing his face.

Kate's heart sank. She had never seen Jake like this. Was it possible he'd met someone else? Maybe he just didn't have the heart to tell her. Come to think of it, the last time they'd spoken, he'd started to tell her something, but she'd cut him off to finish her assignment. Could that have been it?

"I'll call you when I get off," Jake said.

Kate realized that he was waiting for her to leave. It seemed as though the entire restaurant had fallen silent. She spun around and ran out into the street.

Nina couldn't help but feel that everyone was looking at her strangely. *Haven't these people ever seen a Big Mac before?* she wondered.

Lunchtime was when the Weymouth Health and Racquet Club was at its busiest. *If I were working some lame nine-to-five job, the last thing I'd do would be aerobics with the Nazi over my lunch break,* she thought.

It had barely been a week since Nina had started at the health club, but she was already sick to death of it. And it didn't help matters that Zoey was oozing with enthusiasm over any and everything that was health related. At the moment she was skipping lunch to take a yoga class.

Nina sighed. This had been such a bad idea. She'd taken the job all in the name of self-improvement, and, well, she hadn't improved one bit. She was no less of a slouch than she'd ever been, but these fitness fanatics were making her paranoid.

And then there was the fact that she'd barely seen Benjamin at all this week. That was definitely not raising her mood level. *Is this the way it's going to be all summer?* she wondered. *All work, no Benjamin?*

Nina was chewing on a fry and contemplating the sad state of her summer when her supervisor approached her. "Nina," she snapped. "Didn't you read the handbook?"

"Yes," Nina mumbled, trying to swallow quickly.

"Well, Nina, rule number nine is: *Do not eat tempting foods in the presence of clientele.*"

"Oh, yeah." Nina took a gulp of soda. "Sorry."

"Could you please dispose of that?" the supervisor asked, pointing to the mess of McDonalds food and wrappers.

"I guess so," Nina grumbled.

"You *guess* so?" The supervisor glared at her. She looked shocked, as if no one had ever spoken to her in a less than worshipful tone ever before.

Nina stared back at her supervisor. The woman was wearing a skintight orange work-out leotard. Her obviously permed ash blond hair was back in a too tight ponytail. It dawned on Nina that she knew exactly what she had to do. "I guess that you can kiss my butt," Nina said. "Either that or admit that you were wrong to judge my personal lunch preference and snarf down a fry as a token of repentance."

Nina's supervisor had turned a strange shade of dead white, kind of like chalk. Nina turned and walked out before the woman could find the breath to respond.

Aisha held her engagement ring in her hand. *Well, it was nice knowing you,* she thought, staring at the slim silver band.

Aisha clutched the ring tightly as she walked up the steps to Christopher's apartment building.

Her heart was pounding as she knocked on the door.

"Who is it?" Christopher yelled.

"It's Aisha!" she screamed back. "I need to talk to you."

The door swung open immediately, and Christopher rushed out to meet her. "Eesh, I'm so happy to see you." He held out his arms to give her a hug.

Aisha ignored his open arms and instead handed him the ring. "Here," she said bluntly. "I don't want this anymore."

"What?" Christopher said, his mouth falling agape. "Eesh, I mean, I know things have been weird, but d-don't you think this is a little drastic?"

"No, Christopher, I don't." *Don't get upset,* Aisha counseled herself. *Be firm. Be calm. Don't play his game.* "Christopher, I don't want to have secrets, and right now that's all we have. I don't want to be engaged to someone who can't tell me the truth."

Christopher's face seemed to crumple. "Aisha, come inside, at least," he said, his voice fraught with emotion.

"No," Aisha said. She knew that if she met his gaze, she'd start to cry. She'd let him sweep her into his arms, and she'd give up. Let him have it his way. And that wouldn't be fair.

"Eesh, please do this for me," Christopher said in a quavering tone.

Aisha looked inside the apartment. Sitting

196

on the sofa was the girl. When she saw Aisha, she stood up and approached her.

"Hi," she said. Her voice was soft and sweet. She seemed younger than Aisha had realized.

Christopher spun around wildly to face her. He was shaking his head, and he looked angry enough to shake her.

"Hello," Aisha replied.

"I'm Kendra," the girl said, holding out her hand and ignoring Christopher's scowl. Aisha kept her hands in her pockets.

"I'm Aisha," she said bluntly.

"I know." Kendra bowed her head. Aisha looked at Christopher, who shrugged.

"Tell her, Kendra," he instructed finally, slumping down on the sofa.

"I'm Christopher's sister," Kendra said.

"Christopher's sister?" Aisha said, her body filling with relief. "Are you serious?"

"Come here, Eesh," Christopher said, motioning to the space next to him on the sofa. "I'm sorry I didn't tell you about Kendra earlier. I don't know. There are a lot of things we need to talk about."

Aisha looked at him quizzically. "I don't know what to say, Christopher. I mean, you've really put me through a rough week. And I'm still confused."

"Eesh, you've given me a couple of rough weeks in your time," Christopher said softly.

Aisha felt the blood rising to her face. "I know," she demurred. "But still . . ."

"I'll explain everything," Christopher said. "But I need to know . . . are we still engaged?"

"I guess so," Aisha said. "But why would you hide your sister from me? Why would you be so cagey?"

"Give me time, Eesh," Christopher said, clutching her hand. "It's a long story."

Aisha looked Christopher in the eyes. He had forgiven her the David Barnes mishap, and she figured she owed him.

Still, she felt weird. Could it be that Christopher had a secret past?

Twenty

Nina couldn't believe what she'd just done. She walked down the street, sipping the remainder of her orange soda, wondering what to do next. *I guess I'll just go wait for Benjamin,* she decided.

She took the ferry home and walked to the Passmores' house. Even if she had to sit on the stoop and wait for Benjamin to come home from whatever outdoor activity he was doing, she was prepared to do it. After all, it was time for her to take control of her life.

I'm going to talk to him today and tell him what I think, Nina thought. *We should be spending more time together. And now that I've quit my job, we can. Maybe I'll even try surfing.*

When Nina got to the Passmores', she saw that lights in the living room were on. "Hello," she called out. Zoey's parents couldn't be home; they were at work. And she knew where Zoey was—yoga class.

Nina heard moaning. And it was coming from Benjamin's room. *Oh, my God,* she thought. *Something's happened.*

She ran to the door and opened it. Benjamin was lying in the dark, his hands holding his head, a black washcloth covering his eyes.

"Benjamin!" Nina cried. "What happened to you?" Tears welled up in her eyes as she leaned over the bed and looked into his face.

"I—I got into a little surfing accident," Benjamin whispered.

"Oh, my God. Can you see?" Nina felt a moment of sheer mind-numbing terror, as if the floor had opened up beneath her and she was falling. *You willed this on him. You wanted the old Benjamin back, and now you've got him. Are you happy now that you've got him back?*

"It's okay, Nina," Benjamin muttered. "But I—I have this massive headache."

"Oh, Benjamin." Relief flooded into her. "Everything will be okay."

"I think it's just that I've been doing too much," Benjamin admitted. "And I haven't done any of my exercises that the doctor gave me."

"Benjamin, I'll help you with your exercises. It'll give us stuff to do together." She looked at him. He looked so weak, lying there. "Oh, I'm just so happy you're all right," she exclaimed, putting her arms around him.

"I've missed you," Benjamin whispered.

Nina lay down next to him on the bed. "Same here," she said. "Same here."

"Aaron, don't put the whole egg in! Just the whites!" Claire exclaimed.

"Too late now," Aaron said, laughing as he cracked the second egg on the side of the bowl.

"Oh, man." Claire sighed. "Maybe we were being overly adventurous when we decided to make a soufflé."

"We *could* just order pizza," Aaron said.

"Not," Claire exclaimed. "That is not my idea of a romantic dinner for two."

Aaron wrapped his arms around her. "Spending time with you is always romantic," he whispered, his lips just grazing her ear. "I wish we could just stay home all night."

"Well, we can't, Aaron," Claire scolded, removing herself from his grasp. "We have to go to Zoey's graduation party."

"Hmmm," Aaron said. "It's not a common occurrence for us to get the house to ourselves, you know."

"I know," Claire said, kissing Aaron on the

cheek and grabbing for a head of lettuce.

When Aaron and Claire had found out that their parents were spending Saturday night at the ballet, they'd decided to take advantage of the fact that the house was their own. Even Nina was out. She was at Zoey's house, helping her prep for the party.

Claire had thought a romantic dinner would be great. She'd been watching a lot of cooking shows on television lately, and she loved the idea of food as a prelude to romance—candlelight, a gourmet meal, wine. What could be better?

She chopped up lettuce for a salad and instructed Aaron on how to make the vinaigrette. "One tablespoon of oil, Aaron," she called out. When she turned around to see whether he'd done it right, she saw that he'd spilled oil on the floor.

Aaron Mendel was a total culinary disaster. Claire sat down on a stool and put her head on the counter. "Maybe we *should* just order a pizza," she conceded.

"I'm sorry, Claire." Aaron laughed. "I guess cooking is not my forte. Though given some practice, it certainly could be. But at present—"

"At present the only cooking oil in the house is on the kitchen floor," Claire interjected. "And by the way, just what *is* your forte?" she added coyly.

"Let me show you." Aaron kissed her softly on the lips, then more deeply.

Claire inhaled sharply. Why was it that Aaron always had this effect on her? "Aaron, we should do something about food," she murmured.

"Let's leave this dirty kitchen for later and take this into the living room," Aaron said.

He led her to the couch and pulled her gently down on top of him. Kissing him was like being in a dream. Like floating into some other world. Claire barely registered the rustling footsteps outside the front door, the sound of the key turning in the lock. That was all far away. She and Aaron were alone together, and that was all that mattered.

Suddenly the door swung open and a chill breeze swept across the room.

Burke Geiger strode into the room. He stopped in his tracks and stared down at the couch as if he couldn't believe what he was seeing.

Claire gasped. She jumped up so abruptly, she forgot to button the top buttons on her blouse, which Aaron had just unfastened. "Dad," she said. "I thought you were out for the evening."

"No," her father said. "I . . ." He made a strange sort of sputtering sound as if he were struggling to breathe evenly.

"I thought you were going to the ballet!" Claire cried.

"Sarah left the tickets here. We had to come back and get them," Burke said. He seemed to be regaining some of the color that had drained from his face moments ago. "And what—may I ask—is going on here?" He was still standing over them.

"We're just hanging out," Claire began. But when she looked into her father's eyes, she knew it was too late to lie. "We were planning on telling you, Dad," she said softly.

Twenty-one

When Kate got home, the little red light on her answering machine was blinking.

"You have two new messages," the computer voice said.

Kate sighed. *And probably none that I want,* she thought.

She pressed the play button.

Message 1: "Kate, it's Mom. How'd you do on that essay? Please let me know."

"Great," Kate muttered to herself. "I'll be sure to call straight away." She dropped her backpack to the floor as the second message began.

Message 2: "Kate, this is Jake. I wanted to explain about yesterday. The thing is that my boss was—"

The tape cut off.

Just my luck, Kate thought, taking her familiar seat in the armchair.

Kate could hear her mother's voice in her head: *You know what your father says about discipline.* Kate reached into her pocket and pulled out a crumpled piece of paper. It was her essay.

She felt like she was the main character in that book *The Scarlet Letter.* The one who was forced to wear a big *A* around her neck for committing adultery. Kate felt as if the C were branded on her forehead.

She knew she should call Jake. She'd been pretty upset at Burger Heaven yesterday, and maybe she'd misread things.

But calling Jake required energy, which was something she didn't have just then.

Kate leaned back in her chair. Zoey Passmore's party was tonight, and she'd said she was going to be there. But the last thing she was in the mood for was a party.

Kate heard a knock on the door.

"Lucas, I'm taking a nap," she called out.

"Kate, it's not Lucas. It's Jake. I wanted to make sure you were all right. I called, but you weren't around. I've been worried."

Kate got up and came to the door. *God, I must be a sight,* she thought. Her hair was a mass of knots from running around like a crazy woman, and her eyes were puffy from crying.

"Hey," Jake said, walking in. "I was worried. You know, you said you'd go to this party with me, and I couldn't get in touch with you. . . ."

"Sorry," Kate mumbled. "I'm really sorry, Jake," she said.

"Are you okay?" Jake touched her flushed cheeks with his hands.

"Well," Kate said. "I'm better now that you're here."

Jake sighed. "I'm so sorry," he said. "Max freaked out and told me that you were too distracting, that you shouldn't come by work anymore. That's why I was so weird at Burger Heaven. That's why I couldn't talk to you."

Kate almost laughed. Here she'd been thinking that Jake was sick of her, that it was over between them just because of one awkward moment. But that wasn't the case at all. "That's okay, Jake," she said. "What matters is that you're here now."

Lucas's day had been one disaster after the next.

First the boat had run out of oil. Then when Lucas had gone to change it, he'd realized the boat had a broken valve. He'd have to take the boat in for repairs.

It had taken the surly mechanics what seemed like an eternity to find the valve they needed to replace, and, well, by the time he'd gotten back from the shop, he had lost almost a half day of fishing.

Which meant Lucas had had to spend the entire afternoon on the boat in the hot sun.

Lucas was sitting at the kitchen table, eating some macaroni and cheese his mom had made for him, when Zoey called.

Oh, my God, the party, Lucas suddenly remembered as he listened to Zoey on the other end of the line. "You're supposed to be here," she was saying. "What's going on?"

How was it possible that he'd forgotten? It wasn't as though she hadn't been going on and on about it for days now.

Lucas finished up his dinner and went to his room. His legs ached as he walked up the stairs.

He planned to get changed and go right over to the Passmores', but his bed had never looked so appealing before.

I'll just lie down for a second, he thought.

Lucas lay down and shut his eyes. It wasn't two minutes before his half slumber was interrupted.

"Lucas," his father growled. Lucas rose and walked out into the hallway. He stood outside his father's bedroom.

"Yes?" he said.

"You know you gotta be on the boat by five A.M. tomorrow!" his dad screamed.

His dad must be losing it. "Dad, tomorrow's *Sunday*," Lucas called out. He realized it was pointless to argue. "Okay, fine," he said. "Five A.M., it is."

Lucas went back into his room and lay down on the bed again. *Maybe I'll lie back down for five minutes and then go,* he thought.

But in the back of his mind he knew he wasn't going to make it.

Twenty-two

Zoey was pretty content with herself. The entire Weymouth High School graduation class of 1997 had shown up at her party.

That is, of course, with one glaring exception—Lucas. *Where is he?* Zoey wondered. She didn't want to call him again. She'd phoned three times now, and his father had picked up each time. Zoey couldn't stand the thought of bothering Lucas's dad with her trite requests.

He's going to come, Zoey figured. After all, the thought that he, her boyfriend, would *not* come to *her* party . . . well, it was totally outrageous.

Zoey had figured that Lucas would arrive with Kate, but Kate had come on Jake's arm. The two had been inseparable since they'd arrived, talking intimately in a corner of the kitchen.

Maybe he's just taking a long bath or something, Zoey postulated. *After all, he probably had a long day at work.*

"Great party, Zo!" Aisha whispered in her ear.

"I'm glad you're having a good time," Zoey said, putting her arm around Aisha.

"Zo, let me introduce you to Kendra," Aisha said.

So this is the mystery girl, Zoey thought, giving Aisha a quizzical look.

"Zo, this is Christopher's *sister*, Kendra," Aisha said, flashing Zoey a huge smile.

"Oh," Zoey said. "Wow. Well, it's really nice to meet you."

"Thanks," Kendra said. "Thanks for letting me come. I think I'm going to go downstairs and watch the video yearbook that everybody's talking about."

Zoey showed Kendra the way down to the rec room. She could hear the whoops of laughter all the way from the stairs. Zoey could only imagine they were watching the bleeps and blunders part of the tape.

"Zoey, you look amazing," Aisha said, catching her on her way back to the kitchen.

"Thanks," Zoey said. She was pretty happy with her new outfit, which did indeed feature the sunflowered top from the second-hand store. "Is it too much midriff, do you think?" she whispered in Aisha's ear.

"No way," Aisha said. "If you have it, flaunt it."

"If you have what, flaunt it?" Nina asked. She seemed to have appeared out of nowhere.

"Oh, well, if it isn't Little Miss Quitter," Zoey said. "I can't believe you walked out on me."

"Oh, come on, Zo," Nina said. "You *know* it wasn't right for me. I mean, hello, Jenny McCarthy, I'll never be."

"I guess," Zoey said. "Still, it was a good way for us to spend time together."

"Zo," Nina cried. "We'll still spend time together!" She paused. "We'd have more time, of course, if you cut out some of your yoga classes."

Zoey laughed. *Maybe I have been going a little overboard in my fitness regimen,* she thought. *Maybe Lucas thinks so.*

Nina, Aisha, and Zoey stood in silence, surveying the scene. *I should make a career out of this,* Zoey thought as she watched people signing each other's yearbooks, using the sparkle pens she'd bought. *Maybe party planning is actually my calling.*

Nina interrupted the contemplative moment. "Well, if it isn't the creepiest couple this side of the Atlantic," she said. Zoey turned around to see Claire and Aaron walking in.

"What happened to them?" Zoey said. "Claire looks as white as a sheet."

"Maybe she finally realized Aaron's a slime," Aisha muttered.

"Or maybe my dad and Sarah caught them mouth munching," Nina added. "That would bring some drama to the house."

"Oooh," Aisha exclaimed. "That would be awful."

"Speaking of drama," Zoey said. "How good is it that our resident drama queen Lara isn't here?"

"Yeah, thank God for that," Nina agreed.

Lara McAvoy couldn't believe what she was about to pull off.

"Good-bye, Serenity Hills, hello, Chatham Island," she muttered, giggling to herself.

Lara had to be careful not to wake Nurse Esmerelda, who had fallen asleep while doing night duty outside Lara's room. "Bye, Nurse Satan," she whispered while digging into the nurse's white jacket.

Got 'em, Lara thought gleefully, holding Esmerelda's keys in her hand. *I can't believe I didn't think of this before.* Lara tiptoed down the hall, her duffel bag in one hand, her keys in the other.

Lara struggled with the keys. *What kind of*

*a prison is it where they lock you in from the
inside?* she had to wonder.

Finally the door was open, and Lara was
running into the night. She threw the keys
into the grass and practically screamed with
the thrill of it all. She was sober, she was in
control, and she was going home.

Never trust Lara – she's out for revenge. All her promises
make her seem a reformed character, but deep down
she's mad at Zoey for robbing her of Jake. All the island
kids have something to hide. Now there will be no escape
from scheming Lara . . .

Never trust Lara

MAKING WAVES, the hot new series by the author of MAKING OUT

Florida is everything Summer Smith had dreamed of. The sun is scorching, the water is brilliant blue, and the guys are tanned and gorgeous. Will this be her summer of love?